A MURDER AT BRIGHTON

THE KITTY WORTHINGTON MYSTERIES, BOOK 8

MAGDA ALEXANDER

Happily After Publishing

CAST OF CHARACTERS

Kitty Worthington - Our sleuth

The Worthington Family

Mildred Worthington - Kitty's mother
Edward Worthington - Kitty's father
Ned Worthington - Kitty's oldest brother, newly engaged to
Lady Lily
Richard Worthington - Kitty's next oldest brother, currently
in Egypt

The Worthington Household

Grace Flanagan - Kitty's maid
Sir Winston - Family's beloved basset hound

The Ladies of Distinction Detective Agency

Lady Emma Carlyle - Kitty's friend and partner in the Ladies
of Distinction Detective Agency

Lady Aurelia Holmes - Assistant lady detective
Betsy Robson - Receptionist and assistant at the Ladies of Distinction Detective Agency, formerly Kitty's personal maid
Owen Clapham - former Scotland Yard detective inspector, aids with investigations

The Wynchcombe Family and Household

His Grace the Duke of Wynchcombe, Sebastian Dalrymple - married to Margaret, Kitty's sister
Her Grace the Duchess of Wynchcombe, Margaret Dalrymple - Kitty's older sister, now married to the Duke of Wynchcombe
Lady Lily Dalrymple - Sebastian's sister, newly engaged to Ned Worthington

The Litwell Family

Lord Litwell - a marquis
Lady Litwell – his wife
Lord Devon- Lord Litwell's son
Lady Esther – Lord Litwell's daughter

The Harrington Family

Lord Harrington - an earl
Lady Harrington - Lord Harrington's mother
Lady Meredith – Lord Harrington's sister

Other Notable Characters

Chief Detective Inspector Robert Crawford Sinclair from Scotland Yard and Kitty's fiancé

Lord Hollingsworth - A marquis, explorer, and adventurer. Robert Crawford Sinclair's best friend

Lady Melissande - Lord Hollingsworth's sister

Lord Marlowe - An earl. Attracted to Lady Emma

Lady Charlotte Marsh – Kitty's friend. Attracted to Lord Hollingsworth's ship

Lady Gloria Carlyle – Lady Emma's sister. A guest of the Harringtons

Michael Broughton - Assistant Manager at The Majestic

Mister Merton - Brighton Constabulary Superintendent

Constable Brown - A police officer from the Brighton Constabulary

CHAPTER 1

AUGUST 1924

BRIGHTON

*W*ith the social season finally over, our family had journeyed to Brighton to enjoy a summer holiday. Except for Richard, of course. Much to Mother's disappointment, he remained in Egypt playing in the sand and digging up dead Pharaohs as she so colorfully phrased it. A few friends had joined us, but Mister Clapham and Betsy Robson remained in London to handle any matters that presented themselves at the Ladies of Distinction Detective Agency. Not that we expected many. Anyone who was anyone had left town.

We'd reserved all the beach view rooms on the eighth floor of The Majestic, Brighton's most luxurious hotel, with Mother and Father assigned to the largest suite. Not only would it provide our group a place to gather for cocktails before supper, but it would afford us the opportunity to share our daily adventures in a private setting.

My sister Margaret and her husband Sebastian, the Duke of Wynchcombe, had the slightly smaller suite next to theirs. They'd spent most of the season in London, with Sebastian traveling back and forth from Wynchcombe Castle so he could handle estate matters. After this holiday, they would take up residence at Oxford where other duties awaited them, mainly Margaret's chairing an effort to increase the number of women enrolled in that august university and Sebastian's involvement in an organic farming consortium, an issue close to his heart.

Ladies Lily and Melissande, who'd become inseparable during their debut season, had opted to share quarters. Lady Emma, on the other hand, had asked for a private room at the end of the corridor. My brother Ned requested a single room two doors down from Lady Lily. Newly engaged to her, all proprieties had to be observed. Thus, the need for space between them.

Lord Marlowe, however, had no such compunction. He'd asked for the room right next to Lady Emma's. Before he took possession of the room, however, Mother made sure there was no connecting door between the two chambers. Not that she needed to worry. I doubted Lady Emma would agree to a private tête-à-tête with him as their on-again, off-again romance was not faring so well. But hope sprung ever eternal in Marlowe's breast.

Sadly, Lord Hollingsworth could not join us as he was busy outfitting his ship. Although his sailing date was a year away, matters needed to be handled so he could make that deadline. He'd allowed Lady Charlotte Marsh, the latest addition to our circle of friends, to accompany him. Apparently, she was knowledgeable about pistons, whatever those happened to be. To preserve the proprieties—not that Lady

Charlotte gave a fig about them—Lady Aurelia, our third lady detective, had accompanied her. She was curious about the ocean since she'd never seen it firsthand.

My fiancé, Chief Detective Inspector Robert Crawford Sinclair and I were assigned rooms nowhere near each other's. Not that it mattered. As we would have neither Scotland Yard nor my detective agency claiming our time, we planned to spend every waking moment together. A precursor to our wedding day, which would take place in October at St. George's on Hanover Square, this holiday would be the last one as unmarried people we would enjoy with family and friends. I'd hoped the time would be joyful. Unfortunately, it was not turning out as I wished.

For some unknown reason, Margaret had spent the entire train ride finding fault with most everything Sebastian said or did while he'd done his best to placate her. I couldn't begin to guess what had caused her upset as they usually were of one mind.

As to Lady Emma and Lord Marlowe, she'd frowned as soon as he'd boarded the train and responded in monosyllables when he directed a comment toward her. She probably thought he would propose. Again. A useless pursuit since she'd rejected every one of his marriage proposals. She loved him. I was sure of that. But she had a valid reason for turning him down—his refusal to allow her to work as a lady detective after their wedding day. But he wouldn't give up. Somehow, he believed if he asked her enough times she would eventually say yes. He was wrong. Unless he changed his thinking, she never would.

And then there was Lady Melissande who suffered from occasional melancholia. I'd hoped that a trip to the seaside would lift her spirits. So far, it hadn't. But it was only the first morning of our holiday. There was more than enough time for the beach to work its magic. Or at least I hoped it would.

Praying everyone was in a better mood the morning after our arrival, I approached the restaurant table where our group had gathered for breakfast. The entire party was there except for Lady Emma and Lord Marlowe. The night before both had mentioned they would enjoy the morning meal in their rooms. Her reason was easy to discern. She wanted to avoid Marlowe. His, less so. Maybe he was plotting a strategy to get back in her good graces.

Within a few minutes, everyone was served their chosen fare—eggs, bacon, kidneys, sausages, fresh fruit. The waiter was pouring coffee and tea for us when the hotel band struck up a ditty which the singer sang.

"By the sea, by the sea, by the beautiful sea!
You and I, you and I, oh how happy we'll be."

"Don't they have another song they could play?" Margaret asked, her mouth pinched.

"They've only played it twice," Sebastian pointed out in a soothing tone.

"Which is one too many," she huffed.

"Maybe you're hungry, dear," Mother said. "Why don't you try some toast?"

A good suggestion. Margaret had been picking at her eggs, but not really eating them.

"No," Margaret said rather emphatically. "Thank you, Mother. I have no desire for food at the moment."

"Megs, you have to eat," Sebastian murmured in a caring voice.

She tossed him a fulminating glance. "Do I? Do I, Sebastian?" She came to her feet and hurried out of the dining room with Sebastian rushing after her.

"What on earth's the matter with Margaret?" I asked Mother. Normally, my sister was the very definition of level-

4

headedness. But she seemed to be currently mired in an emotional storm the likes of which I'd never seen.

"She's feeling a bit under the weather, dear."

"Really?" I glanced in the direction my sister had taken. "She seems all right to me." Except for her bad temper.

"It comes and goes. I imagine she'll be right as rain by this afternoon."

I scrunched a brow. What sort of illness affected one in the morning but resolved by the afternoon? Whatever it was, I hoped Mother was right. I would hate for Margaret to be ill the entire time we were in Brighton.

Lady Mellie was staring off into space, her mouth turned down at the corners. Unfortunately, her melancholia was making itself known. It had not been apparent during the season when she had balls and routs to attend. But now that those events had ended, she had nothing to keep her mind occupied. I'd hoped a seaside visit would lift her spirits, but unfortunately, she seemed to be sliding back.

Lady Lily's newly engaged status to Ned did not help as they only had eyes for each other. Lady Mellie was happy for them, I was sure. But she missed the close friendship she'd enjoyed with Lady Lily whose world now revolved around Ned.

There was no help for it. It would be up to me to fill the void. "Would you like to visit the pier after breakfast, Lady Mellie?"

She gazed out one of the windows. "Do you think the weather will hold? It appears to be threatening rain."

Storm clouds were gathering in the horizon. "How about a game of cards?"

She scrunched her face. "Not my favorite activity." She brightened up. "I could play the piano. They have one in the guest lounge."

"No," I said rather emphatically. Whenever she turned

melancholic, she played dirges. Nobody wanted to hear Beethoven's *Requiem* during a summer holiday. "We could visit the Brighton Royal Pavilion. Robert could escort us." I turned to my fiancé. "Couldn't you, darling?"

"Of course, whatever you wish," he agreed with an easy smile.

"We could make a party of it. Would anyone else like to come along?" I glanced pointedly at Ned and Lady Lily. When neither answered, I spoke up, "Ned!"

"Yes?" He pried his gaze from his intended.

"Would you like to join us after breakfast? We're visiting the Brighton Pavilion."

He turned to Lady Lily before answering, "How does that sound, sweetheart?"

"It should be fun." Her glance toward Ned grew down-right adoring.

Heavens! Did I ever look at Robert with such a nauseating gaze?

Seemingly reading my thoughts, he whispered in my ear. "They're in love."

"I never look at you that way," I whispered back.

He tilted his head to the right. "Well . . . "

"Horrid man!" Dismissing him, I turned to my parents. "Mother, Father, would you like to join us?"

Not for a moment did Mother hesitate. "Afraid not, dear, I have letters to write."

"Father?"

"I, ahem, have some correspondence as well."

He was a horrible liar. Father didn't have personal correspondence. And as for business, he had staff for that. Obviously, he and Mother wanted to enjoy some private time. I bit my lip to keep from laughing. Who was I to deny them a bit of pleasure? "Next time then."

CHAPTER 2

THE ROYAL PAVILION

*T*he Royal Pavilion was built as a royal residence for George, the Prince of Wales, who later became King George IV. The magnificent palace, heavily influenced by both Chinese and Indian fashion, was used as a seaside retreat by his royal highness who spent a jolly time entertaining, and being entertained by, his mistress, Maria Fitzherbert. Although he'd subsequently married her, the marriage had been deemed invalid. She was a Catholic, and the Royal Marriages Act prohibited such a union.

The Royal Pavilion had not been a favorite of Queen Victoria, however. After railroads linked Brighton to London, the seaside resort had become extremely popular. Her Royal Majesty, who abhorred crowds, had eschewed the Royal Pavilion and set up her own summer residence, Osborne House, in the Isle of Wight. It was far enough from Brighton to satisfy her desire for privacy.

Our little group, less exalted beings that we were,

immensely enjoyed the pavilion, especially Lady Mellie who could not stop praising the palace architecture. "Wasn't it divine, Kitty?" She asked on our way back to our hotel.

"Divine indeed." As I hoped, the trip to the pavilion had indeed worked its magic and she was once more the pleasant young lady we all dearly loved.

We arrived back at The Majestic to find a lady berating an unfortunate front desk clerk. "I specifically asked for a room with a view of the ocean, young man. But my suite is in the rear of the hotel, and it overlooks the town. That is unacceptable."

"My apologies, Lady Litwell. We are simply bursting at the seams," the hapless clerk explained while putting on a placating smile. "I've checked our upcoming vacancies. A suite with a view of the beach will become available in three days' time."

"That will not do! I need that suite now. Make it happen."

"Now. Petal, I think that—"

Lady Litwell peered down her quivering nose at the gentleman whose head barely reached her shoulder. "Lucius, nobody cares what you think. Least of all me." She brushed a theatrical hand across her brow. "I've developed a headache. I'm going back to my room."

Lucius started to follow, but she stopped him. "That dog needs a walk," she pointed to the Pomeranian held by Lucius on a leash. "And when you return, don't bring her to my chamber. I don't want it shedding all over me."

"Yes, Petal."

"Don't. Call me. That," Lady Litwell bit out before turning her back on the gentleman.

He gently picked up the Pomeranian and walked out the front door carrying the pooch, seemingly fighting back a grin.

"What an unholy terror," I murmured to Ladies Lily and Mellie. Both nodded in unison.

Robert and Ned soon rejoined us. They'd gone to fetch our room keys from the unfortunate clerk who'd suffered through Lady Litwell's harangue.

"That was downright atrocious, the way Lady Litwell talked to the desk clerk and the gentleman."

"The gentleman is her husband, Lord Litwell," Ned said.

"Really?"

"Just so."

How very humiliating. His wife had addressed him as if he was nothing more than a lackey. "How do you know them?"

"Worthington & Son handles their funds." The investment firm Father and Ned owned and managed as equal partners. "Lady Litwell inherited a sizable fortune from her first husband, a diamond mine magnate from South Africa who died several years ago. Shortly after her arrival in England, she asked us to invest her inheritance. Within a week or so, she married Lord Litwell."

I would have loved to inquire further, but I would not get any more out of Ned. The information he'd shared was bound to be public knowledge. Anything else would be confidential. He valued his client's privacy too much to reveal such things.

"Mother left word for us," he said waving a note. "Our supper reservations are for eight. But she'd like us to gather in her and Father's suite at seven for cocktails."

Leave it to Mother to organize the entire group. Something I truly appreciated for I had no desire to worry about anything. I only wished to enjoy myself in Robert's company. "Well, it's three now," I said, glancing at my watch. "Enough time to take in a nap before dressing for supper."

"That would be lovely," Lady Lily said. "I'd like to rest before dancing tonight."

One of the better known attractions of The Majestic was its excellent band. Lady Lily, indeed all of us, had developed a love for popular music after visiting Gennaro's, London's famous jazz club.

While Ned escorted Ladies Lily and Mellie to their rooms, Robert accompanied me to mine where my maid Grace was waiting for me. "You haven't been here all day?" I would have hated for her to be cooped up inside when the seaside beckoned.

"Oh, no, Miss. I had a lovely walk down to the shore. Those bathing houses are so odd. People enter in their day garments and then emerge in their bathing suits. I also stopped by the pier," she said almost conspiratorially, "and enjoyed something called a hot dog. Why, Miss, it's nothing but a bit of sausage in a bun. It was rather tasty, though, I must say." Once she'd helped me out of my dress and into a robe, she asked, "What time would you like me to wake you, Miss?"

"Six. I'd like to bathe before cocktails at seven." By the time Grace finished drawing the drapes, I'd fallen asleep.

Things had not changed much by the time we gathered for cocktails. Lady Emma was still not speaking to Marlowe, and Margaret and Sebastian remained at outs with each other. But we'd had one triumph. We'd succeeded in lifting Lady Mellie's spirits. So much so, she was busy rattling off to Mother about the lighting in the Royal Pavilion, even going so far as to suggest Mother could adapt the same illumination for the music room. Rather than brush off her suggestion, Mother seemed to take to the idea. Not a surprise. She loved to redecorate. Before long, Mother was making plans to visit the Royal Pavilion so she could see it for herself.

Father, who happily indulged Mother in her redecorating

schemes, simply shook his head while mentioning his purse growing lighter.

Of course, we had news of our own to share—mainly Lady Litwell's tirade over her inferior rooms.

Mother, who kept abreast of all matters regarding the nobility, filled us in on the lady. "Her first husband died six years ago in South Africa from a venomous snakebite. Shortly after his tragic death, she traveled to England."

"She wasted no time shaking the dust from her feet," I said.

"Indeed. She came from common stock—not that there's anything wrong with that. But having become a wealthy woman, she intended to marry a titled husband. Lord Litwell fit the bill perfectly. A fifty something widower with a vast estate to support. Land rich, cash poor. Rumor has it she arranged the marriage before she left South Africa."

"How very efficient of her," I said, sipping my cocktail.

"Unfortunately, he's not quite what she envisioned in a husband. He prefers a quiet life in the country, while she likes the gaiety of the city. He favors his estate while she craves being the one in the limelight. Being the self-centered creature she is, she resents the attention he showers on anything other than her."

"That resentment was very much on display this morning. Lord Litwell had a Pomeranian with him. His wife wanted nothing to do with it."

"Does he, by Jove?" Father asked. "He didn't mention it when we took him on as a client."

"Do gentlemen normally discuss such personal details, Edward?" Mother asked.

"You'd be surprised what they mention, my dear." He waggled his eyebrows.

"Gentlemen can be such horrid creatures," my strait-laced mother murmured.

"Ah, but you love us all the same." He wrapped his arms around her and kissed her cheek.

Mother pinked up. "You do have your benefits."

I loved to see them in this playful mood. I could only hope my marriage would enjoy such wonderful moments.

"It's a few minutes to eight," Ned said glancing at his pocket watch, "shall we head down to the restaurant?

"Oh, yes," Lady Lily said. "I must admit I'm starving."

"It's the sea air, dear," Mother said. "It has a bracing effect on appetites."

Except for, strangely enough, Margaret who normally enjoyed a healthy one.

With our party being as large as it was, we'd reserved a table. Neither too close to the dance floor, nor the kitchen, it was, however, within easy reach of the balcony so we could enjoy the ocean breeze. One did need to have a shawl handy as the night air tended to cool things a bit.

After our server took our orders, Lady Mellie continued to expound about the beauty of the Royal Pavilion. Once that subject was exhausted, I announced Robert and I would head to the shore in the morning. By ourselves. After waiting an age to witness his manly physique, as it were, I neither desired nor needed company to enjoy the view. My announcement was met by smiles and dare I say a snicker from an unidentified source—Lord Marlowe.

Eager to turn his thoughts in another direction, I asked him, "What are your plans for the morrow?"

"I thought to invite Lady Emma for a stroll along the pier or—"

"Emma!" A female voice called out, interrupting what he was to say next.

"Gloria!" Lady Emma exclaimed once she'd caught sight of the speaker. The young lady who'd hailed her was her sister who'd made her debut this year. With her fair complexion and mahogany tresses, she was quite similar in coloring to Lady Emma. Unlike Lady Emma who was quite serious, she was a jolly sort, intent on thoroughly enjoying life.

Once they exchanged cheek kisses, Lady Emma introduced her to the group. Not that she needed to as most of us had met her in the London ballrooms.

"How do you come to be here?" Lady Emma asked.

"Lady Harrington invited me. And here she is with her daughter, Lady Meredith." Lady Gloria pointed to the two ladies who'd followed her trail. The younger one had to be Lady Meredith as she clearly numbered the same years as Gloria. The older one had to be Lady Harrington. Close to Mother in age, she appeared very frail as she walked with a cane while leaning heavily on her daughter's arm. "May I introduce them?"

"Of course," Lady Emma responded.

Once the introductions had been performed, Lady Harrington said, "Indeed, dear Lady Gloria and my own Meredith have become bosom bows. Merry, as we call her, refused to travel to Brighton unless her dear friend came along as well."

"That's awfully kind of you, ma'am," Lady Emma said.

"They make me feel years younger with their antics . . . and older." She laughed. Clearly, she adored both young ladies. "I can barely keep up with them. Oh, and here's my son, Harrington."

Tall, blonde, with a certain charm about him, Lord Harrington had inherited the title from his father a mere three years ago. I'd met him last spring during my debut. He'd been one of the rare ones who didn't pay the slightest attention to me. With his fortune, title, and extremely good looks, he'd been much in demand. But at the end of the season, he'd issued no wedding proposal to any of the debutantes who'd hoped for such a thing. Rumor had it he was a serious sort of gentleman, much devoted to his mother and sister after his father passed away and had no time to properly court a lady. Whether that was true was anybody's guess.

After introductions were once more made, he bowed over Lady Emma's hand. "How very fortuitous to meet you again, Lady Emma."

"Oh?" she said apparently surprised.

"I asked you to dance two years ago at Lady Crofton's ball."

"I do believe you're right Lord Harrington. How very amazing you remember."

"You made quite an impression on me." His blue eyes were alight with merriment. "I looked for you this season, as I wanted to renew our acquaintance. But alas I could not find you." In a dramatic gesture, he held his open palm over his heart as if it pained him.

"I've been rather busy, milord," Lady Emma said. "Miss Worthington and I own a detective agency. I'm afraid there is not much time to attend balls."

One of his brows hiked up. "Do you, by Jove? How very interesting. You'll have to tell me all about it. Tomorrow morning after breakfast? We can take a walk to the pier."

Marlowe, who'd been quietly seething during the entire exchange, cleared his throat.

Taking the hint, Lady Emma said, "I'm afraid I have plans for tomorrow morning." She beamed Lord Harrington a smile. "But my afternoon is quite free."

"Capital! Let's say two. I'll wait for you in the lobby. If that's amenable to you, that is."

"It is," Lady Emma said with a grin.

Before any more gnashing of Marlowe's teeth occurred, the maître d' thankfully broke into their conversation, "Sorry to interrupt, milord. Your table is ready."

"Oh, yes, of course. If you would excuse us." After bowing over Lady Emma's hand, he offered an arm to his mother. With his sister and Gloria trailing in their wake, they followed the head waiter to their table.

As of one mind, Mother and I jumped in to veer the subject away from the Harringtons. Do I even need to mention Lord Marlowe fumed the rest of the meal?

CHAPTER 3

A CURIOUS CONVERSATION

*T*he following day I visited the Royal Pavilion. Again. I would have declined as I was eager to enjoy some time alone with Robert. But when Mother expressed an interest in spending time with me, I acquiesced. It would be the last holiday I would have with her as a single lady. In two months' time, I would no longer live at Worthington Manor, but at Robert's Eaton Square address. It was a small sacrifice to make for a mother who'd given me the world.

As I wanted to visit the hotel shops before we went on our way, I strolled down early to the lobby. Once I'd done so, I settled into one of the wing chairs and waited for the rest of my party to join me. Unfortunately, I witnessed yet another tirade of Lady Litwell. This one was a rather nasty exchange between her and a young lady I quickly surmised was her stepdaughter.

"Can't you do anything with your hair, Esther? It rather resembles a rat's nest."

"I try, Stepmama. But there's so much of it."

She did have a point as her tresses reached past her shoulders to her mid back. A trim by a good stylist would do wonders for it, but it appeared she hadn't had it cut in quite some time.

"The humidity from the beach wreaks havoc on it," the unfortunate Lady Esther further explained. "There's no managing it."

"Then have your maid cut it into a bob, for heaven's sake. It's all the rage, after all."

"Unfortunately, Sadie is not up on the latest styles."

"That maid of yours is totally useless. Did she even take a flat iron to your dress? It's full of wrinkles."

"I don't know." Poor Lady Esther looked like she was close to tears.

"Well, at least you have a decent complexion. But you must stay away from the sun if you want to keep it that way. Husbands don't desire a brown sparrow for a wife."

Lady Esther got a mulish look to her face. "I don't want to get married. I'm only seventeen."

"Balderdash. Plenty of young ladies marry at your age or younger. Now what do you have planned for today?"

"Oscar wants to go sailing."

"And how would your brother manage that? He doesn't own a sailing vessel."

"Yesterday he met a man who owns a boat. He offered to take us out on the water. For a fee."

"Of course. Nothing is free in this world as I have good cause to know." Lady Litwell seemed to have momentarily lost herself into a remembrance of some kind. An unpleasant one going by the bitter twist to her lips. But in the next

17

moment, she snapped back to the here and now. "Do you have a hat?"

Esther held up the one in her hand—a cloche which looked as if it had seen better days.

"For heaven's sake, child. Where's your common sense? You need a sunbonnet."

"I don't have one, Stepmama," Lady Esther whispered in such a soft tone I barely heard her.

"The hotel shops are bound to have some. Get yourself one."

Lady Esther seemingly could do nothing right as far as her stepmother was concerned. She did have that English milk and rose complexion, which was lovely, but her height was not remarkable. Having inherited her father's stature, she barely came up to her stepmother's shoulder. She was dressed for the beach in a short-sleeved dress that reached her knees, but neither the color, a drab brown, nor the style did her any favors. "Yes, Stepmama."

"Stop calling me that."

Lady Esther kept mum. No wonder. If she spoke, her stepmother would just snap at her.

Lady Litwell seemed to realize she'd gone too far. "Well, nothing we can do about that at the moment. Stop by my room when you return. I have a lotion for the sunburn you're bound to have."

"Yes, Step—." She stopped herself before she could proceed further but then she brightened up when she caught sight of someone. "Oh, here's Oscar."

Had to be her brother as their resemblance to each other and their father was quite remarkable.

"Good morning, ma'am, Esther." He kissed his sister's cheek but merely nodded to Lady Litwell. He probably knew better than to address her as Stepmama.

"I understand from Esther you're going sailing."

"That's right." The smile never left his lips. He was not as easily cowed as his sister.

"Who with?"

"A chap I met yesterday. He has a sailing boat."

"One that's for hire."

"Of course."

"And where are you going to get the funds to pay for it?"

"I had a bit of good luck at the tables, so I'm flush at the moment."

Lady Litwell's face fell. She enjoyed having them at her beck and call. The fact that Oscar didn't have to depend on her to have a good time at Brighton seemed to chafe her. But she bounced right back. "Ummm, easy come, easy go."

"Oh, I don't think it'll go anywhere," the nasty smirk to his lips seemed to be a good adversary to Lady Litwell's maneuvering. Turning to his sister, he said, "Ready?"

Lady Esther nodded.

"If you'll pardon us, ma'am," he said to Lady Litwell, and then with his sister in tow he led the way out of the lobby into the summer sunshine.

Lady Litwell didn't waste any time turning to her next victim, the hapless desk clerk. "Young man!"

"Yes, Lady Litwell."

"I don't suppose a beach view room has opened up."

"No, ma'am."

"Umm, the service in this hotel is downright horrid. I'll make sure to let all my acquaintances know." And with that she flounced off.

I shot the desk clerk a commiserating smile but did not have a chance to say anything as my mother and the others were approaching.

❧

THE NEXT MORNING, I woke bright and early vowing nothing would keep me from carrying out my plans. As Robert and I planned to head for the shore, I didn't want to go through the bother of dressing properly for the restaurant. So rather than join my family for breakfast, I chose to enjoy it in my room.

A little before nine, I stood in the lobby awaiting his arrival which gave me time to witness yet another exchange between the fractious Litwells. This time it was the siblings who were engaged in a less-than-amicable conversation. Honestly, couldn't they find a private spot to conduct their disagreements?

"Come on, Esther. We'll have fun," Oscar pled with his sister.

She turned a cold shoulder to him. "No, thank you, Oscar. You hoodwinked me yesterday. Something I did not appreciate. I ended up having to pay for the boat rental. That's half of my beach allowance gone. Besides, I have no interest in going sailing at night. There's nothing to see."

Poor thing. I truly felt sorry for her.

"I'm not exactly flush at the moment," Oscar explained.

"Because you gambled it away. You get three times my allowance from Father."

"You live at home. I don't," he said in a peevish tone.

"Nobody asked you to remove yourself."

"I can't be expected to live there. Not with that harridan in residence."

"Stepmama is not so bad, Oscar."

I'd seen the way Lady Litwell treated her. Not for one second did I believe that statement.

And apparently, neither did her brother. "Oh, cut line, Esther. She's always harping at you about your hair, your complexion, your figure. She's never pleased."

"She only wants me to present at my best so I can attract a gentleman's attention."

"Fine. Have it your way. I'll just have to figure something else out." And with that he stormed off.

Poor Lady Esther looked like she was about to cry. I thought to offer a word of comfort. But before I could do so, she gathered herself and headed toward the lift.

"Woolgathering?" A deep voice asked close to me.

Robert! His sudden appearance drove every thought from my head. Spectacularly attired in beige linen trousers and a matching short-sleeved shirt, he'd left the shirt's top two buttons unfastened. My fingers itched to run my hands through the hint of dark chest hair that peeked through. "Not exactly."

"We should have a grand time. It's a beautiful morning."

I tossed him a saucy smile. "Yes, it most certainly is."

CHAPTER 4

A VISIT TO THE SHORE

*B*righton, located as it was on the southern part of England by the English Channel, boasted of summer breezes which regularly welcomed those who traveled from London. One of the more endearing sites along the beach were the colorful bathing boxes that lined the shore. We'd rented one of them for the duration of our visit so we could have a place to change from our day garments to our bathing suits. Since our family had made other plans, Robert and I had it all to ourselves.

Being the gentleman that he was, Robert allowed me to change from my summer frock to my bathing wear, a bright blue swimsuit—in the latest fashion of course—which reached to my upper thighs. I must say I felt quite daring in it, for I'd never exposed that much skin before. While Robert changed into his bathing suit, I plopped a sunbonnet on my head and sat on one of the beach chairs conveniently located on the hut's porch to catch the summer breeze.

I did not have long to wait for Robert to emerge. When he did, he took my breath away. His modest bathing trunks covered all the important bits, but his upper shirt revealed much more than I anticipated. Strong, muscled arms, more of that tantalizing chest hair and . . . scars. Of course, there'd be scars. He'd been seriously injured, not once, but twice. Once in the line of duty when he'd saved Lord Rutledge from a gang of thugs in one of London's worst areas, and again during the Great War. How had I not expected them?

My amazement must have shown clearly on my face, for he said, "Not quite the knight in shining armor you were expecting."

"Oh, Robert," I said, my hand softly caressing a particularly grievous-looking scar that ran down the side of his torso and wrapped around to his back. "You are, and always will be, my knight in shining armor." Not caring we were in public view, I pulled him down and kissed him fully on the mouth.

Although he enthusiastically reciprocated, he ended the kiss rather abruptly. Taking my hands in his which had not ceased their exploration of his magnificent physique, he said, "We should stop before you excite me beyond what's acceptable."

"Oh," I blushed. Having obtained an education on the male anatomy from my sister Margaret, I knew what he meant. "Very well. But I intend to continue my quest on our wedding night."

He flashed that charming smile of his. "With my full blessing, my darling Catherine."

Holding hands, we made our way down to the beach where we spent the next hour cavorting in the waves. Robert proved to be a strong swimmer. While I was not up to his level, I held my own as Mother had made sure all her children knew how to handle themselves in the ocean. We spent another hour strolling along the shore. I'd been foresighted enough to bring a small bucket so I could collect seashells. Not only would they make a wonderful memory of this wondrous day, but I would paint them a watercolor version of them on my journal. When the sun rose directly overhead, we returned to the beach hut as Robert had arranged for a light luncheon to be delivered. After a quick rinse at one of the council-provided showers, we changed back into our day clothes. Soon, we were enjoying sandwiches, a quite delicious punch, and a fruit dessert.

"I'm rather sleepy now," I said once I'd finished. The not unexpected result of exuberant exercise and a meal.

"Shall we head back to the hotel?"

"I hate to, but I think we better. I'd like to have a proper bath and a lie in."

After tossing our meal remnants into a conveniently located bin, we made our way back to the Majestic where we discovered a message from our party. They'd returned from their outing. As we would see them soon enough, we headed to my room where Robert kissed me goodbye. We would only be apart temporarily, as we'd meet for cocktails at seven.

I entered my room to find a message from Mother. "Come to my suite as soon as you can."

"Do you know if anything is wrong?" I asked Grace. Servants knew everything.

"Well, Miss, apparently there was a disagreement."

"Lady Emma and Lord Marlowe?"

She shook her head. "Their Graces."

"Margaret and Sebastian?"

"Yes, Miss. Apparently, Her Grace was not feeling quite the thing, and His Grace insisted she return to the hotel."

"And it went on from there."

"Yes, Miss."

I rushed through my bath and slipped into a boat neck orange top with short sleeves and a white skirt with buttons along the side. Soon, I was knocking on Mother's door. I'd expected her to be alone, but Margaret was there . . . crying. That horrified me. Margaret never cried. "What's wrong?" I asked.

"Nothing," Margaret cried out. "Everything is fine."

All evidence to the contrary.

"Go talk to your sister," Mother said. "I ordered tea." The solution to every ill.

"I don't want bloody tea," Margaret exclaimed.

"Language, please," Mother admonished. As far as she was concerned there was never a call for that word.

"I apologize," Margaret said.

I joined Margaret on the settee. "Dearest, tell me what's the matter. I want to help."

She raised a tear-stricken face. "I'm with child."

Unable to comprehend the enormity of what she was saying, I gazed around the room. Finding no diminutive person nearby, I asked, "What child?"

"Kitty," Mother said, shaking her head.

"I'm pregnant," Margaret said before dissolving into sobs and falling into my arms.

CHAPTER 5

A SURPRISING REVELATION

"What? How did that happen?" I asked.

Margaret stopped crying long enough to toss me a look that branded me an idiot.

I quickly redeemed myself. "Well, of course, I know how it happened. You provided quite an exhaustive explanation of how that is achieved while I was in Oxford. But you take precautions."

"Clearly, they didn't work, Kitty," my loving sister bit out through clenched teeth.

Heavens! She was in a mood.

"Dearest," Mother said, taking a seat on the other side of Margaret. "While dear Margaret and Sebastian made their plans, God decided otherwise. This child is a blessing."

"I know that," Margaret said, teary-eyed. "But 'tis not what I planned. I have the chairmanship of the Oxford Committee to increase enrollment of women, and my fundraising causes to manage. How am I going to get it all done with a baby on the way? And after the baby is born?"

"Oh, pshaw, Margaret," I said. "If there's a lady who can achieve great things and then some, that's you. You juggled your wedding, studying at Oxford, sponsoring Ladies Lily and Melissande during the season. A babe might slow you down—"

"I don't wish to slow down. I wish to achieve things."

"There's nothing more worthy of achievement than a child," Mother said.

"But how am I going to get through this pregnancy? I'm sick all morning long. Can't hold down any food until the afternoon. If that were not enough, my energy is flagging. I tire from simply taking the lift down to the restaurant. All I want to do is sleep."

"All perfectly normal, dear," Mother said, patting Margaret's hand. "But those symptoms will abate in a month or so. In the meantime, you will need to adjust your activities, of course. Sleep late. Have a light meal in the morning. Toast and tea worked wonders for me. Once you feel up to it, you can rise, maybe take a stroll along the beach with Sebastian. After another afternoon rest, you can join us in the evening for supper."

"But I have a million things that need doing. The Oxford Committee is counting on me for ideas and plans."

"Margaret, you can do that while resting," I said. "All you need is a notebook and a pencil."

"But the university expects me to do things, not just write down ideas."

"Dear, you're not the only one on this committee," Mother said. "Surely, there's at least one person you can delegate matters to."

"What about Letitia Fairbright?" I suggested. We'd met her during a murder investigation at Oxford. "She volunteered to help. She's certainly capable. You can ask her to be your co-chair."

"She's taken on additional responsibilities at her Oxford college. I'm not sure if she'll have the time."

"I doubt she'll turn down such an offer," I said. "It's a feather in her cap to be part of this committee. It's bound to improve her standing at the university."

She gave one final sniff and blew her nose. "Maybe you're right. I'll write her a letter detailing my proposal."

"That's the ticket," I said.

"And after Oxford, you'll be spending time at Wynch-combe Castle," Mother said. "The castle staff will cosset you so much you won't have to lift a finger. They'll be over the moon about the impending birth of an heir."

"It's just as likely to be a girl."

"Whom everyone will dote upon," I said.

"And then it will be Christmas once more," Mother said. "A joyous celebration either at Wynchcombe or in London."

"Wynchcombe Castle. Nothing like it for the holiday. A grand Christmas feast, raising that huge tree once more, decorating it, dancing, and wassail." Margaret was growing more excited by the minute.

"I hope we're invited," I said. Last December's celebration, which had included her wedding, had been truly memorable.

"Of course, you are. I want my entire family around me."

"And then a return to London for the baby's birth. In February?" Mother asked.

Margaret nodded. "I believe so, yes."

"We'll have to arrange for a physician here in Brighton to examine you. If only to ensure everything is proceeding smoothly."

"Yes," Margaret gazed down at her hands. "But first I must apologize to Sebastian. I've been rather horrid to him."

"Yes, you have," I said.

28

"Kitty!" Mother admonished.

"Well, she has, Mother. No sense beating about the bush." I glanced back at Margaret. "It takes two people to make a baby, and you've been blaming him."

"Unfairly, I know. He's always so careful." She breathed out a soft sigh. "I hope he forgives me."

"Serves you right if he doesn't!"

"Kitty, you're not helping," Mother exclaimed.

Margaret laughed. "Yes, she is. Thank you, dear sister." She gave me a quick hug. "You always know the right thing to say."

"You're welcome. But honestly, you have nothing to worry about. There's nothing Sebastian wouldn't forgive you."

"Shall I ring him, dear?" Mother asked, pointing to the telephone.

"No." Taking a deep breath, Margaret came to her feet. "I'll go to him. Do you think he's in our room?"

"Probably wearing out the rug."

A small giggle escaped Margaret. "He does like to pace."

"Shall I accompany you?" I offered.

She frowned as if she found the suggestion offensive. "It's right next door. I can manage." And then, head held high, Margaret walked out of the room.

Once she stepped out, Mother and I rushed to the door and opened it just a smidge to hear what would be said.

As soon as Margaret knocked on her door, it opened. "Megs," Sebastian sounded dreadful.

"I'd like to apologize for my behavior. I hope you'll forgive me."

"Oh, my darling." And then their door closed and there was silence.

Mother and I both sighed as she gently shut her own.

"Well, that was . . ." I said.

"Exactly."

"She's really pregnant?" I asked.

"I believe so. She's certainly showing all the signs."

After giving birth to five children, Mother would certainly know.

"Well, now that we've handled that crisis, I best return to my room. I'd like to have a bit of a lie in before cocktails."

But as I walked down the corridor, one thought niggled my mind. If Margaret could get pregnant as careful as she and Sebastian had been, what hope was there for me?

CHAPTER 6

TROUBLED SEAS AHEAD

*M*argaret and Sebastian wasted no time in making their big announcement. During cocktails, he tapped a glass to get everyone's attention. Once he had it, he gently wrapped an arm around Margaret's waist as if she was made from porcelain. "Margaret and I would like to share our wonderful news. "We're anticipating a happy event."

Everyone gathered around them to offer their congratulations. "Oh, my goodness. A baby!" Lady Lily said. "How are you feeling?"

"Suffering from a bit of morning sickness," Margaret answered, "but Mother tells me it will pass soon."

"I can't wait to be an aunt!" She turned to Ned. "And you'll be an uncle."

Ned shook Sebastian's hand and kissed Margaret on the cheek. "My most fulsome felicitations. You'll make a wonderful mother. After all, you had the best."

"Oh, get on with you," Mother said blushing. "I only did what had to be done."

Lady Mellie's turn came next. "I don't know what I could do. I've never been around children." But if I can be of any help, please do not hesitate to ask." Given that she was raised in a convent, it made perfect sense.

"Why, Mellie, you can play the baby a lullaby or two," Margaret said.

"Or compose one!" Lady Lily suggested.

"You can compose music?" I asked.

"I don't flaunt it about, but yes."

"That would be a perfect present for the baby," Margaret said, pressing Lady Mellie's hand. "His or her own lullaby."

Father moved forward next. "So, you're making me a grandfather."

"I'm sure you'll spoil the babe."

"I certainly will." His grin was one of the biggest I'd seen on him.

Lady Emma and Lord Marlowe offered their felicitations which left Robert for last.

"My heartiest congratulations."

"Thank you," Sebastian said. "Mayhap you'll be a father next. Once you marry Kitty, that is."

"That's not happening for a long, long time," I said. "Not the wedding, the baby." I didn't want anyone getting any bright ideas.

Margaret laughed. "That's what I said, and yet"— she rubbed a loving hand across her belly— "here I am."

The merriment continued through supper. And then the band, which had been playing soft background music, struck up a fox trot and a couple of professional dancers took the floor for a dance demonstration. After the dance ended, the gentleman asked an older lady to dance while the young woman approached a gentleman seated by himself. Soon they were swaying to a waltz. Knowing how much I enjoyed dancing, Robert held out his hand. Much as everything else, we were very well suited as both of us loved to dance. After the waltz ended, we returned to our table just in time to watch Lord Harrington approach Lady Emma.

"May I have the honor of this dance, Lady Emma?"

"She can't," Marlowe interjected. "She's dancing with me."

"No, I'm not." Lady Emma said coming to her feet. Lord Harrington wasted no time leading her to the ballroom floor.

Marlowe sat fuming the entire time they were dancing. As soon as they returned, he shot to his feet. "A word, Harrington."

"Marlowe, whatever you're thinking of doing, don't!" Lady Emma exclaimed.

Ignoring her, Marlowe pointed toward the balcony which stood beyond the open doors close to us. "Outside."

"Oh, dear," Mother said.

It wasn't long before heated words reached us.

"You have no right to lay hands on Lady Emma. Not with your reputation."

"What are you going to do about it?"

"This."

When the sound of fists striking flesh reached us, Robert shot to his feet and headed for the balcony. Sebastian stood as well but, glancing at Margaret, he paused.

She wasted no time urging him to follow. "Go!"

Poor Lady Emma's face had turned downright red. She was that embarrassed. Understandably so. She was not the kind of female who enjoyed men fighting over her. She probably wanted to hide under a rock. But she remained steadfast until Robert and Sebastian returned.

"Marlowe will not be returning," Robert said.

"Lord Harrington?" Lady Emma asked.

"He's taking a few moments, but he plans to come back."

Thankfully, the occupants of our table were the only ones who'd noticed something had gone awry as everyone else in the ballroom was enjoying themselves. Thank heaven for small favors. The servers who'd attended to us had not missed a thing, however. Both returned with complimentary bottles of champagne. Never let it be said that The Majestic did not treat their guests right.

Fifteen minutes later, Harrington breezed into the room, not a hair out of place, although there was a suspicious bruise on his left cheek. Thankfully his beard disguised most of it. He stopped by our table and engaged in desultory conversation with Lady Emma about the air in the balcony being too brisk. And then he excused himself and rejoined his party. His mother and sister as well as Lady Gloria apparently had missed all the excitement because they were all smiles when they greeted him.

Lady Emma, however, was not smiling. Claiming a headache, she excused herself for the evening. As soon as she did, Lady Mellie declared herself exhausted after the long day and linked arms with Lady Emma. Soon, they were heading off to their rooms. More than likely Lady Mellie's 'exhaustion' stemmed from a kind heart. She didn't want Lady Emma to go off on her own. But she had no need to worry. One of us would have escorted Lady Emma to her room.

For the next hour or so, we pretended nothing had happened, but of course it had. Our party broke up early— Margaret and Sebastian being the next to retire with Mother and Father next. Ned and Lady Lily decided to visit the hotel lounge where a pianist was serenading guests. It allowed them to conduct a conversation in public while enjoying their closeness.

Brisk weather or not, Robert and I headed for the balcony. There was a full moon after all. After I wrapped my shawl around me, we braved the outdoors. If it grew too cold, well, I could always depend on Robert to put his arms around me and keep me warm.

"What happened?" I asked when we reached a spot far enough from the open doors so no one could overhear us.

"By the time Sebastian and I reached them, Harrington was on the ground. Stands to reason. Marlowe was a pugilist at Oxford so he knows how to box."

"I can't believe he'd strike another man simply because that gentleman asked Lady Emma to dance."

"I sensed there was more to it than that. According to Sebastian, Harrington attended Oxford at the same time as Marlowe. Something must have happened during that time which put Harrington in an unfavorable light."

"Do you know what it was?"

"No. It was after my time at Oxford. I've never heard of anything against Harrington. But then I don't keep abreast of the comings and goings of the nobility. Sebastian knows nothing as well."

"It could have been something as simple as both being interested in the same young lady. Marlowe certainly resents Harrington's interest in Lady Emma."

"Maybe."

I shivered.

"You're cold." He started to take off his jacket.

"No." I wrapped my arms around his waist and stepped into him. "I have another idea for you keeping me warm."

His kiss and embrace were everything that was wonderful, but we couldn't indulge for long. If someone strolled into the balcony, we could be discovered. And we wouldn't want that.

"Maybe we should step back inside," I suggested.

He tweaked my chin, a tender gesture of his. "Once we're

married, we won't have to separate. We'll have all the privacy we need."

"It cannot come soon enough for me."

He walked me to my room where we spent more delicious time saying goodnight. When I slipped into my chamber, I found a note from Lady Emma.

"Come to my room. No matter how late. I need to talk to you."

My wristwatch told me it was a little after eleven. After taking a walk to her room, I knocked on her door. When she opened it, there were clear tracks of tears on her face.

I embraced her in a warm hug. "I'm so sorry, Lady Emma."

"Thank you," she said after a few moments. "Shall I ring for tea?"

"The kitchen is closed by now."

"Yes, of course." Sighing softly, she took a seat on the settee in her room. "I know what I have to do. Problem is, I don't want to do it. I fear I must, though," she said clenching her hands.

Clearly, she was troubled. "What did you have in mind?"

"Breaking up with Marlowe."

Taking a seat next to her, I pressed her hands. "You were never attached to him, dearest."

"Not officially, no. The problem is I love him."

Even though I'd known it, she'd never admitted it before. "I suspected you did."

"I've been rather obvious, haven't I?" Lady Emma asked, somewhat chagrined.

"Any lady would fall for him. He's handsome, intelligent, and has made it abundantly clear that he's attracted to you. Never mind he has a title and a fortune."

"Yes, he is all that. But I can't countenance his behavior. He likes to be in control. He doesn't want me to be a lady detective. And now he can't even bear for another man to ask me to dance with him. What would he be like once we married?"

I said nothing as there was nothing I could say.

She raised a tear-filled gaze to me. "But I must do it. There really is no other choice. I need to make a clean break of it."

"I'm so sorry, Lady Emma."

"Could you please call me by my first name."

"Of course, dear Emma."

She let out a shuddering sigh. "I'll write him a letter, slip it under his door."

"Whatever you think is best. Shall I leave you to it?"

Emma nodded as she wiped another tear from her cheek.

"If you need anything, anything at all, just ask."

She hugged me. "You've always been the best of friends, Kitty. I'm so glad I found you."

"So am I. Now, try to get some sleep. After you write your letter, of course." She wouldn't be at peace until she had.

CHAPTER 7

A PLAN THWARTED

*W*hen I joined my family and friends for breakfast the following morning, I didn't know what to expect. Would fireworks erupt between Marlowe and Lady Emma or would they pointedly ignore each other? Would they even join us for breakfast or enjoy the meal in their respective rooms?

At least one of those questions was soon answered as Lady Emma arrived the very depiction of sadness. Not only did she have dark circles under her eyes, but the sparkle was missing from them. Anticipating she would feel most comfortable seated next to me, I'd made room for her there. And then the entire party waited on bated breath for Marlowe to make his appearance. We didn't have long to wait.

He strolled into the restaurant, dressed to the nines in his best coat. Shoes shined, immaculate tie neatly knotted. Sporting that fabulous grin of his, he took a seat on the opposite side of the table from Lady Emma. "I'm starving. Anyone up for a sail after breakfast? I believe we can rent a runabout at the marina."

Margaret's face turned a sickening shade of green. "Excuse me." Jumping to her feet, she took off, probably in the direction of the nearest loo.

Marlowe was immediately contrite. "I'm sorry. I didn't intend—"

"No need to apologize, Lord Marlowe," Mother said. "With Margaret being in a delicate condition, such an endeavor might not appeal to her."

Thankfully, a server soon arrived to take our orders, smoothing over the unfortunate moment. While another waiter served tea and coffee, Marlowe and Lady Emma studiously avoided so much as glancing at each other. At least we did not have to worry about Lord Harrington as neither he nor his party were present.

After the meal, Marlowe and Lady Emma went their separate ways. She to read a book she wanted to finish; he to go sailing by his lonesome as no one joined him in his endeavor. As Robert and I had decided we wanted to head for the shore once more, we proceeded to our respective rooms to change into different attire.

As I'd already slipped into my bathing suit underneath my frock, it was just a matter of removing the dress, and tossing on my stylish beach robe. The day before I hadn't been daring enough to wear it. But after noticing several ladies sporting similar garments as they strolled along the shore, I felt it would be acceptable for me to do so. I reached the lobby before Robert which gave me once more a front row seat, if you will, to the trials and tribulations of Lady Esther. She was at the front desk asking about Oscar.

"I'm looking for my brother. He's in room 308. I knocked on his door, but he didn't answer. He went sailing last evening, and I'm worried about him. Has he claimed his key?"

"One moment. Let me check." The desk clerk searched the cabinetry where the room keys were kept before addressing Lady Esther once more. "The key to room 308 is still here."

"So, he hasn't returned?" Her face was filled with worry.

"I can't say. But I've been on duty all morning, and no one has asked for that key."

"Oh, dear."

"Would you like to write a note? I can make sure he sees it when he claims the key."

"Yes, thank you."

"Ready?" Robert. He'd suddenly materialized next to me.

I'd been so mesmerized by the front desk drama I'd missed his approach. But I made up for it immediately. Flashing Robert a smile, I curled my hand around his elbow. "To go off with you? Always."

He took the bag in which I'd stored a change of clothes and towels from me. "That's a rather ravishing beach robe you're wearing, Miss Worthington."

"Why, thank you, Inspector." I shaped my mouth into a moue. "And they say men never notice."

"I do my humble best, my dear."

I squeezed his arm. "And you do it beautifully." He was once more attired in linen trousers, buttery yellow this time, and a matching short-sleeve shirt. The tantalizing peek of that manly chest of his made me, well, damp, shall we say?

"What had you so enthralled you didn't notice my approach?" He either hadn't noticed my state, or like the gentleman that he was, chose to not mention it.

"Lady Esther." After we made our way out of the hotel, I related what I'd overheard today as well as the argument from the day before.

"He'd gone sailing, you say?"

"Well, that was his plan yesterday," I said. "I don't know if he managed it as he was short on funds. Apparently, he gambles quite a bit."

He frowned. "There is a myriad of ways a young, titled lord would spend an evening. He'll probably return sometime today. I wouldn't worry unduly about it."

"You're probably right."

"If Lady Esther wants to worry about something, it's her brother's gambling that should concern her. That's a horrible addiction. It's ruined many a family."

"Esther mentioned his allowance was three times hers. But he countered with the need to pay for his bachelor quarters."

"A London flat can be expensive, but it can be managed. I lived in one on a police officer's salary. Most nights it was beans and toast for supper."

"You didn't live with your parents when you served in the London Metropolitan Police Service?"

"I should have. But young fool that I was I wanted to prove my independence."

"Where was the flat located?"

"East London."

I shuddered. That area of London suffered many air raids during the Great War. If he hadn't joined the war effort, he might have been killed. But then, he almost was. Wanting to shift the conversation to a happier topic, I said. "And now you're living at a posh Eaton Square address with a staff that waits on you hand and foot."

Recognizing my wish for levity, he quipped. "They will do the same with you."

"Will they?"

"Oh, yes. They can hardly wait to serve the great lady detective. Well, the female staff, anyway."

I scrunched my nose. "You're teasing, Robert."

He stopped our progress and gazed at me. "Truly, I'm not. It's not so hard to understand, Catherine. You've succeeded in a field which normally is occupied by men. That gives other women, including my own staff, hope."

"I never realized that," I said after we'd resumed our walk. "And I did not succeed at the investigations by myself. Family and friends, and you, have helped a great deal."

"But you're the one the papers mention."

I shook my head. "I've never wished to court that notoriety."

"That's what makes it so intriguing to the newspaper reporters and the public. If you flashed it about, they would pay no notice to you."

"Uggh, I hate having my name bantered about in the dailies. But I refuse to give up the lady detective business. I enjoy it too much," I said.

"No one expects you to, darling. Least of all me."

"Thank you for saying that. I truly appreciate your support. I just wish other men felt the same way."

We walked a few more steps before he said, "Marlowe and Lady Emma were rather studiously avoiding gazing at one another this morning. Do you know what that was about?"

"Lady Emma ended their relationship, such as it was. She wrote him a letter."

"Ahh, that explains that forced air of gaiety about him."

"All a facade, I'm sure. He's devastated."

"How do you know?"

"When she said she was going off to read a book, his gaze . . . it broke my heart. He's deeply in love with her, and she with him. If only . . ."

"You can't cure all the ills of the world, Catherine."

"I know. Still." I shook off the sadness. "I'm glad he's gone sailing. It will give him an opportunity to lick his wounds without us witnessing his misery."

"Well, here we are." Robert said as we'd finally reached the beach hut. Retrieving the key we'd been given from his trousers pocket, he inserted it into the lock and turned. But when he pushed, the door would not give. His brow knitted. "That's strange. It seems to be stuck."

"Push harder." I joined him in this endeavor, and soon we discovered what had been blocking the door.

Lady Litwell. She lay seemingly in repose, eyes wide open, and very much dead.

CHAPTER 8

DISASTER

"*N*ot again!" I exclaimed.

Bending down, Robert put his fingers to Lady Litwell's neck and felt her pulse. A useless endeavor. Her head was bent at an impossible angle. Still, he had to check.

"She's dead, isn't she?" I asked.

He straightened up. "Afraid so."

I let out a heavy sigh. "We can't even take a holiday without tripping over a body."

"I'm sure Lady Litwell would much rather be alive."

"Yes, well, that ship has sailed."

His lips quivered at my unintended quip.

"We'll need to notify the local police, I suppose," I said in a lugubrious tone.

"Yes. But one of us should stay here to preserve the scene."

"I'll go find a police officer." No way would I volunteer to stand sentinel over Lady Litwell's remains.

"There's a police station halfway between here and the hotel."

I'd noted it on our stroll to the beach hut. "I'll return as soon as I can." And then I was off. Thankfully, the officer on duty, Constable Brown, did not flinch when I notified him about what we'd discovered. He simply put on his police helmet and followed me back to the hut. When we arrived, Robert introduced himself and provided a succinct account of what he'd observed.

"Chief Inspector, Sir. It's an honor to meet you." Clearly, Constable Brown was impressed by Robert. "Wish it was under pleasanter circumstances."

"Unfortunately, it is what it is," Robert said. "You'll need to contact your superintendent. He'll want to get an inspector here as soon as he can. We'll wait until he arrives."

"I'll get right down to it. Thank you, sir."

Officer Brown made a great show of rushing back to the police beach station. But it took another half hour for him to return. The news was not good. "Sir, there might be a problem getting an inspector here. He was rushed to the hospital with some kind of emergency."

"You only have one detective inspector?"

"No, Sir. We have two. The other one is on his honeymoon in Spain."

When Robert glanced off into the distance, I could almost read his thoughts. He was considering getting involved in this case. "No, Robert!" I said. "No."

"Catherine." He placed gentle hands on my shoulders. "Someone must handle the preliminary investigation. Once that's done, the Brighton superintendent can request help from another constabulary. Maybe even from London."

"You're from London, sir," Officer Brown enthusiastically pointed out. "I'd be dead thrilled to have you lead the investigation."

I tossed him a dirty look.

"You're not helping, officer," Robert cautioned Constable Brown.

"No, sir. Sorry, sir. Another police officer should be here in a short time as well as the medical examiner."

"He's not on vacation also, I hope?" I asked. If he was, that would create a huge problem, as there would be no one to establish the cause of death.

"Oh, no, ma'am. He never takes one. Lives for the job, he does. Why there was this one time—"

Robert interrupted, "We're returning to The Majestic, Constable. That's where we're staying. I'll call the constabulary and talk to your superintendent. Stay here until the other officer and the medical examiner arrive."

"Yes, sir. Thank you, sir."

On our way back to the hotel, I argued my point. "You're not taking this case, Robert. There are plenty of other inspectors who could do it. They can get one from somewhere else."

"Chances are other constabularies are short on staff as well. Most are on holiday."

"You're on holiday!" I emphatically pointed out.

"Yes, but I'm here. I know the victim."

"You saw her for two minutes, if that."

"But you saw her for a longer time *and* overheard the conversation with her stepdaughter and stepson."

"Oh, no. You're not getting me involved in this. We have enough drama within our circle of family and friends."

"Maybe a nice murder investigation will get their minds off their woes." He accompanied this outrageous statement with a charming smile.

I huffed out a heavy sigh. "You're impossible."

"But you love me all the same."

"Well, yes, there is that." He would point that out.

I needed to clean myself off. The beach was a wonderful place, but it tended to attract a lot of sand. So, once we reached The Majestic, I headed to my room. Grace wasn't there. Of course, she wasn't. She probably thought I'd spend all day at the beach. I peeled off my clothes, gathered my toiletries, and rushed through my bath. Half an hour later, I knocked on Robert's door. He was dressed immaculately in one of his business suits.

"Well?" I asked. He'd mentioned he'd be calling the head of the Brighton Constabulary.

"Superintendent Merton wants me to handle the investigation."

"Of course, he does." The Brighton superintendent would be an idiot not to request the assistance of a Scotland Yard chief detective inspector.

"He'll be here in an hour. I have to telephone my superior at Scotland Yard and square things with him. Would you care to wait?"

That conversation could take a while as he would need to be connected to London. "No. Thank you."

"Very well. What are you planning to do?"

Mother was out of the question and so were Margaret and Sebastian. "I'll visit Lady Emma and see how she's faring."

"Good idea. Shall I knock on your door in an hour? We can enjoy a luncheon at the Grotto." One of the hotel restaurants. I had to give him credit. He was trying to salvage what he could of our holiday.

"That would be lovely," I said in a much pleasanter tone of voice.

After saying goodbye to him, I headed off to Lady Emma and was fortunate enough to find her in her room.

"Kitty! Back already? I thought you were planning to spend the day at the shore with Robert."

I explained what we'd found.

"Lady Litwell dead! Now there's a turn up." I could see the wheels clicking in her head.

Robert was right. The investigation would take her mind off her troubles.

"So how did she die? Do you know?"

"Her neck was at an odd angle. I think it may have been broken."

"It would take a great deal of strength to achieve that. But what was she doing in our beach hut? And how did she get in? It was locked, wasn't it?"

"Yes, it was. There must be more than one key. Several, I imagine. It's a rental after all. Someone must have gotten a hold of one of them."

"Was the corpse fresh?"

"No. It was rather ghastly. She was a sickening shade of blue. Robert surmised she must have been dead at least twelve hours going by the state of the body."

"What time did you arrive at the beach hut?"

"Around eleven."

"So, she had an assignation with someone around midnight."

"Maybe."

"Was she, er, fully dressed? She wasn't interfered with?"

"I can't speak to that issue. The medical examiner will have to provide that information. But she didn't appear to have been as she was fully dressed." I glanced at my watch. Somehow an hour had almost gone by. "I have to leave. I'm meeting Robert for lunch."

She pulled a notebook from the desk, excitement clear on her face. "Shall I keep thinking of questions?"

Robert was right. This murder had given her something to think about other than her own misery. "Yes, do that."

CHAPTER 9

A REQUEST IS MADE

*A*fter Robert found me in my room, we headed to The Grotto, the seaside themed restaurant within the Majestic. Painted in shades of blue and green and decorated with all manners of marine flora and sea life on the walls, it provided the illusion you were part of the ocean.

We ordered the special of the day, fillets of sole lightly breaded in flour and pan-fried in butter, with a ratatouille accompaniment and crusty bread rolls. Our wine choice was a crisp Sauvignon Blanc.

While we ate, he shared his conversation with his Scotland Yard superior. "He approved my assistance in the investigation."

"Of course, he did."

"He did say the time spent on the investigation would be counted as work, not a holiday."

"How very noble of him." I couldn't help the snarky tone to my voice.

He reached out across the table to capture my hand. "I know this is not what you want, Catherine. But I am an officer of the law. It's imperative this case be handled well and quickly."

Swallowing my disappointment, I offered him the best smile I could muster. "Make sure to mention that when you request time off for our honeymoon. However many days you spend on this investigation, we'll tack on to our time in Paris."

Raising my hand to his lips, he kissed it. "Thank you for understanding."

"You're welcome, Inspector."

By the time I was enjoying the mousse au chocolat, I was immensely grateful we'd managed to carve this time together. From past experience, I knew we would not have many more moments like these.

Just as we were finishing our desserts, a gentleman approached us. He was attired in a jacket emblazoned with his name on the pocket. Clearly, a hotel employee.

"My apologies for interrupting your meal. I'm Michael Broughton, Assistant Manager at The Majestic. Do I have the pleasure of addressing Chief Detective Inspector Crawford Sinclair?"

"I'm he, yes," Robert answered.

In a very low voice, Mister Broughton said, "Superintendent Merton from the Brighton Constabulary is here. He's informed us of an unfortunate incident that happened in one of the beach huts. He kindly requests a moment of your time."

I glanced at Robert. "And so it begins."

"Yes, of course." Robert came to his feet. "Would you like to join us, Catherine? I suspect he'll want to talk with you as well."

I was not about to desert him. "Of course."

Addressing Mister Broughton, he said, "Please have the waiter put the meal on my account, Room 810."

"No need to do so. The meal will be the compliments of The Majestic," Mister Broughton said while leading the way out of the restaurant. "I hope you understand. We would very much like to keep The Majestic out of this unfortunate incident."

"Yes, of course," Robert said.

Mister Broughton showed us to a private room, located far enough away from the entrance so the hotel guests would not notice.

Inside, a gentleman stood. Quite distinguished-looking, tall, with dark hair, he appeared to be in his early fifties.

As soon as we stepped into the space, he held out his hand toward Robert. "Thank you for joining me, Inspector Crawford Sinclair. I'm Superintendent Merton."

After greeting him, Robert performed a quick introduction. "My fiancée, Catherine Worthington. As we both discovered Lady Litwell's body, I assume you'd want to talk to her as well."

"Yes, of course."

The room was small but elegantly appointed. It contained a sofa, a settee, and two chairs all upholstered in an aqua and blue chintz pattern, which reflected the colors of the sea. Robert and I had barely accommodated ourselves on the sofa when a waiter arrived with coffee and tea service and a fruit and cheese platter. "Compliments of The Majestic," he said as he placed the tray on the table in front of Robert and me.

Given the preferential treatment, it was clear the assistant manager wanted The Majestic kept out of the investigation. Couldn't blame him. The last thing a hotel wanted was to be associated with a murder. Whether that could be accomplished was anybody's guess.

After the waiter left, I played Mother and served the

superintendent and Robert. While we ignored the food platter—we'd just enjoyed our luncheon, after all—the superintendent availed himself of the cheese and fruit. "My apologies. I missed my luncheon. You don't mind?"

"Of course not," I said.

"If you could tell me how you came across the deceased."

Robert and I related the details.

"And the beach hut was locked?"

"It appeared to be, yes," Robert said.

"There's no other way out?" The superintendent asked.

"There didn't appear to be."

"So whoever murdered her must have had a key," the superintendent said.

"Either the person she met had one or she did," Robert said. "Had to be a duplicate."

"Yes, it would appear so," the superintendent slowly rolled out his words. "Unfortunately, not every beach hut key is returned which is why their owners charge a key replacement fee up front."

"So anyone who'd rented that beach hut could have kept it," I said.

"And made an assignation with Lady Litwell," the superintendent said. "That would be my guess. Have you informed Lord Litwell about his wife's death?"

"No. I thought you'd want to take the lead on that," Robert said. "It would be more official coming from you. Speaking of that, how would you like to proceed?"

"This case will need to be handled with kid gloves. You have a great reputation for solving cases. Especially in those dealing with members of the upper class. It's a great imposition as you're on holiday. But I truly appreciate your help."

"I've discussed it with my superior at Scotland Yard. He's approved my assistance with this matter."

"I also telephoned him as well. I'm glad we're on the same page."

"So, what would you like to do next?"

"Well, for starters, I suggest you accompany me to Lord Litwell's room. Not only would I like your take on him, but you can address any questions he may have."

"Yes, of course. May I suggest Miss Worthington join us? If she's amenable, that is."

"Whatever you think is best," I said.

The superintendent appeared befuddled by Robert's suggestion. "I'm sorry. But what would be her purpose?"

"Miss Worthington has been involved in several murder investigations in London and been successful at every one. You may contact Scotland Yard if you wish to make enquiries about her level of expertise. Additionally, Miss Worthington overheard several conversations between Lady Litwell and her husband as well as her stepchildren. So she's somewhat familiar with the family. And being a lady herself, she can offer a woman's point of view."

"Well, if you think that's best." Superintendent Merton did not appear entirely convinced about my participation in this investigation. More fool he.

"What would you like from me after we've talked to Lord Litwell?"

"If you could report to me on a daily basis, I would appreciate it. The investigation is bound to attract quite a bit of attention, so I'll arrange for a press conference tomorrow afternoon. I'll let you know so you can attend."

He wasn't an attention hog like Robert's Scotland Yard superiors. How refreshing. Of course, if the case went sideways, then Robert would be to blame.

"Do you have any other questions?" Superintendent Merton asked.

"The postmortem?"

"Should be done by the time of the press conference. I'll inform you of the results as soon as I learn them."

"Do I have access to any resources?"

"An officer, do you mean?"

"Yes. I might be in need of one."

"Constable Brown is eager to be assigned to the case. He quite admires you."

"He'll do."

CHAPTER 10

A CONVERSATION WITH LORD LITWELL

*L*ord Litwell showed no emotion when Superintendent Merton told him about his wife's death. Having witnessed his wife's treatment of him, I didn't expect sadness. Nor would he be jubilant, as that would show bad form. But I did anticipate a sense of relief. After all, he would no longer have to put up with the harridan. But his expression did not change in the least. And that in itself was surprising.

"Do you know of anyone who desired Lady Litwell's demise?" Superintendent Merton asked.

Lord Litwell measured his words carefully. "She was a rather difficult person to deal with, so people tended to avoid her. But no one threatened her, if that's what you're asking. And as far as I know, she didn't receive any correspondence to that effect."

"What about your relationship with Lady Litwell? Was it amicable?"

"We rubbed along as well as could be expected."

"Would you care to explain?"

"As I mentioned, my wife was a difficult woman. She found fault with everything and everyone, including me. I was polite to her." As he spoke, he stroked the fur of his pomeranian which had taken repose on his lap. She seemed happy enough to lay there. "We had our disagreements, but I would never hurt her."

That was left to be determined. He wouldn't be the first husband who killed a troublesome wife.

"Where were you last night, say between ten and two in the morning?"

"Why, right here. After supper I took Miranda for a walk."

"Miranda?"

Lord Litwell pointed to the pomeranian. "She's my truest companion."

"I . . . see." The superintendent murmured. Obviously, he was not a lover of dogs. "And after your walk?"

"We returned around nine or so. She stays with me."

"You do not put her in the kennel?"

"Miranda does not approve of that arrangement. And, frankly, neither do I."

I didn't blame him. Father would keep Sir Winston with him if he could. But Mother would never allow such a thing.

"Can anyone confirm you were indeed in your room during the times I mentioned?"

"Afraid not, Superintendent."

"Lady Litwell was a very rich woman." The superintendent had done his homework. "Who inherits her fortune?"

"I haven't the foggiest. Strange, I know. But it was not something we discussed."

"How can that be?" The superintendent didn't begin to understand Lord Litwell's situation.

"Before we married, we came to a financial arrangement

which she fully met. With the funds she settled on me, I was able to satisfy the debts of my estate. Thanks to some very savvy investments, I'm now comfortably off. If matters proceed as they have in the last few years, my modest fortune should continue to grow."

His message was clear. He did not need to murder his wife as he had enough for his needs. Still. He could be making the thing out of whole cloth. It was something that would need to be investigated.

"You did not wish for a divorce?"

He paused stroking the dog's fur. "No. Maud and I married with two objectives. She got to be Lady Litwell; I got to save my estate. If I divorced her, I would be reneging on our agreement. It would not be an honorable thing to do."

"Love was not part of the bargain, then?" The superintendent asked.

"No."

"You called her Petal," I said.

He allowed himself a small smile. "You heard that, did you?"

"In the lobby reception area."

"My little rebellion, you might say, Miss Worthington."

I understood what he meant. "She hated for you to call her that, so of course you did."

"It was all that I could do."

No, he could do a lot more like murder his wife. Maybe he'd finally been fed up with his wife's behavior toward him or his daughter. But the beach hut location did not make any sense. How would he have drawn Lady Litwell there? What excuse would he have used? After all, if he wished to have a private conversation with her, he could have easily held it in his room or hers.

"What about her relationship with your children?" I asked taking over the interview.

He lost his smile. "She was very critical of them, especially Esther. I was very displeased and discussed it extensively with her." He issued a heavy sigh. "It didn't do any good."

"And your son?"

"Oscar by and large ignored her jibes, although I must admit some of her criticism was deserved. It was just the way she went about it that was unconscionable."

"How so?" I asked.

"More often than not, she tended to show her displeasure in public. Something I strongly disapproved of. But again, there was no curtailing her words."

"Would he have acted against her?" I asked.

"Oscar only acts when something gives him pleasure or benefits him. Her death would have done neither. I doubt she named him as a beneficiary."

"But you said you don't know the terms of her will."

"I don't and neither does he. He wouldn't act in such a manner on the off chance she left him some money. No. That would not make sense."

"What about Esther?"

"Esther is not the most assertive of individuals. My fault, I'm afraid. After her mother died, I focused on saving the estate. I paid little attention to her, choosing to leave her in the care of her governess. The woman encouraged Esther to be submissive. It's only in recent years, she's begun to show some spirit. But she reverts to submissive when confronted by a stronger personality."

"Like her stepmother."

"Yes."

"How long were you planning on staying in Brighton, Lord Litwell?" Robert asked.

"We were scheduled to be here for another week, and then we planned to return to my estate in the Cotswolds. Maud had arranged a house party for early next month. We'll need to cancel that now." He glanced at the superintendent. "There will be an inquest, I suppose."

"Yes, once we receive the medical examiner's findings," the superintendent said. "I would think tomorrow or the next day. I will inform you of the date. In the meantime, don't leave Brighton."

"No, of course not."

"Do you know where your children are to be found at the moment?" Robert asked.

"Esther will probably be in her room. She usually rests in the early afternoon. I have no idea about Oscar."

Interesting. So Oscar had not appealed to his father for funds.

"We'll need to talk to them. Would you like to inform your daughter about her stepmother's death?"

"Yes, I think that would be best."

After coming to his feet and telling Miranda to stay, he led the way to a room at the end of the corridor.

Lady Esther opened the door wearing a robe over her undergarments. Clearly, she'd laid down for an afternoon rest. "Father!" she exclaimed clutching the robe.

"My dear, may I come in. I'm afraid I have some rather sad news."

Her breath hitched. "Not Oscar."

"No."

When she opened the door wider to let her father in, I was able to peek into the interior. The room was very small, with barely enough space for the bed, a small wardrobe, and a night table.

Five minutes later, he emerged. His daughter was getting dressed and would soon join us.

While we waited, we spotted Mister Broughton making his way toward us. Turned out he had a message for Superintendent Merton. "My apologies for interrupting. Sergeant

Ames telephoned. He would like for you to call him. He said it was rather urgent."

"Right. Forgive me, Lord Litwell. I must attend to this."

"Of course."

"Inspector Crawford Sinclair will take over the investigation. He has my full support and confidence." He turned to Robert. "I'll be in touch as soon as I'm able."

"Of course." And then Superintendent Merton followed Mister Broughton to the lift.

We didn't have long to wait for Lady Esther. She emerged dressed in the same frumpy brown dress I'd seen on her before. Lord Litwell may have spent funds on his estate, but clearly he dedicated little money to his daughter.

As we couldn't very well question her in the hallway, we retraced our steps back to Lord Litwell's room where we accommodated ourselves.

Lady Esther's interview did not shed any light on the matter. The day before she'd gone for a walk on the beach with her maid. They'd visited the pier. But as she had little money to spend, they soon returned to the hotel. She'd enjoyed a light luncheon in her room and then had a bit of a lie in. She'd joined her family for supper at the restaurant and then returned to her room where she spent the evening reading. Apparently, this was her normal routine. Much like Lord Litwell, no one could attest that she'd spent the crucial hours surrounding the murder in her room. But then I didn't expect anyone could. She seemed to lead a very lonely existence.

CHAPTER 11

WE ADVANCE IN OUR INVESTIGATION

*O*nce we left Lord Litwell and his daughter, we headed toward Lady Litwell's room. Located several doors down, it was quite larger than her husband's. Much like my parents' suite, it was more luxuriously appointed.

There was a front room, a sitting room, and a huge bedroom with a huge tester bed draped in ocean hued curtains. Lady Litwell may not have spent any money on her stepdaughter's room, but she'd spared no expense for her own quarters. The only thing missing was the view. While my parents' room faced the ocean, hers looked out into the city of Brighton. Interesting though it was, it did not hold a candle to the beach vista.

"How would you like to go about this?" Robert asked me. The sitting room contained, much like my parents', a sofa, a settee, and several chairs, a console table, several side tables and cabinets, all in the Art Nouveau style with curving lines and organic shapes. Lighter in color and not as heavy as the

Georgian period, the furnishings communicated an air of elegance and beauty which suited the holiday atmosphere of the hotel.

The huge bedroom did not disappoint. Much as my parents', it connected to a dressing room and an en suite bath.

"I can explore the bedroom. Why don't you take the sitting room?"

"Very well."

Twenty minutes later we'd found nothing of note. Lady Litwell had not kept a diary. The only thing that was interesting was a desk blotter which provided a hint of some words, but none of them provided a clue. Several bottles of medicine rested on the vanity table in the dressing room. I made a note of them in the journal I'd brought with me. She had quite an array of beauty products, expected for a woman who prized her beauty. Most were of French and Italian origin, but there was one perfume that seemed to have been made especially for her since it was labeled with her name. I gave the bottle to Robert and suggested he have it analyzed. On the side table next to the bed, I found a cache of sleeping powders. Several were missing. She must have taken them to help her sleep. There was no alcohol anywhere in the suite. The lady was not a drinker. The dressing room contained a safe. That showed promise. We would need to get the hotel to open it for us.

The cleaning staff had already been in the room so sadly all the bins had been emptied. "We'll need to talk to the cleaning lady. They might have noticed something important."

"Maybe. Or maybe not."

It was early days. Sooner or later, we would find something that would point us to the murderer. Or at least I hoped it would.

After Robert and I left Lady Litwell's room, we headed for Mother and Father's suite. I wanted to inform them about the peeress's death and Robert's handling of the case before they found out from other sources.

"Kitty! Oh, and dear Robert," Mother said when she opened the door. "How was your day at the beach?"

It was wonderful, except for the part where we discovered a dead body. I couldn't very well say that, so I simply asked, "May we come in?"

"Of course."

I glanced around the room. "Where's Father?"

Her mouth pruned with disapproval. "He's taking Sir Winston for his afternoon constitutional. Why he himself takes that dog for walks when there's perfectly good hotel staff to handle that chore is beyond me. We did pay extra for the service."

"He loves Sir Winston, Mother."

"Yes, well. Never mind." She'd developed a thorough dislike of Sir Winston after he'd suffered a grievous mishap on our priceless dining room carpet.

"We have news. Not good ones I'm afraid," I said, hoping to soften the blow.

"Oh."

"Lady Litwell is dead. She was murdered."

"Oh, dear," Mother said. "But how do you know?"

"Unfortunately, we found her in the beach hut," I explained.

"The one we rented for our stay?" Mother asked horrified.

I nodded.

"That's unfortunate. I imagine you have a story to tell. Shall I order afternoon tea?"

"An excellent idea." While we enjoyed the spread which

consisted not only of tea but scones, sandwiches, and all manners of treats, Robert and I related the rest of our news.

"So dear Robert will be in charge of the investigation?"

"Afraid so, ma'am. It's not how Catherine and I wished to spend the holiday."

"But duty called," Mother said, "which, of course, you had to answer."

"Yes, ma'am," Robert said.

I admired him for his devotion to duty, but I wished it didn't come calling so often. Father returned while we were enjoying the repast. Once he heard the news, he was just as appalled as Mother.

"In the beach hut we rented. That's downright unconscionable," he said. "How did they even get in?"

"That's something we'll need to find out," Robert said.

CHAPTER 12

COCKTAILS AND MURDER

*W*hen our entire party met for cocktails in my parents' suite, Robert announced Lady Litwell had been murdered, and he was taking on the investigation.

Same as Father, Ned zeroed on the most logical question. "But how did they gain access to the beach hut?"

"According to the front desk, people don't always return the keys so there could be several not accounted for. Although anyone experienced with breaking and entering could have easily picked that lock." After our afternoon tea, Robert had wandered down to the lobby to see what he could discover about the beach hut keys.

"Yes, well, there is that," I said.

"The Majestic can't possibly be in charge of handing out keys for all the beach huts," Father said.

"They're not. But apparently, the owner of this particular one only rents to those staying at The Majestic. He doesn't want undesirables, as he calls it, utilizing his property."

"So if The Majestic has exclusivity, the staff would know who rented that particular bathing box?" Ned asked.

"Yes," Robert said. "While I was questioning the front desk clerk, Constable Brown officially reported to me. He's been assigned to help with the investigation. I asked him to discover the names of the individuals who rented the huts for the last six months or so and determine if any keys were not returned."

"I was thinking—" Lady Emma said.

"A good thing," Marlowe interrupted.

Lady Emma quelled him with a look. Once he'd been effectively silenced, she proceeded, "One of the first things we should investigate is Lady Litwell herself. Who was she dealing with that wanted her dead?"

"Absolutely," I said. "But we'll also need to find out about her finances. Ned? Can you shed any light on them?" Now that Lady Litwell was no longer among the living, the law took precedence over anything else.

"Are you planning to involve everyone in another murder investigation?" Mother asked in dismay. "Robert, I understand. He's a detective chief inspector at Scotland Yard, but not the rest of you. We're on holiday."

"You're right, Mother, but we would welcome all the assistance we can get." I glanced around the room. "Of course, it will be up to everyone to decide if they wish to participate." Even though I thought I knew their answers, I asked, "Who's in?"

Everyone but Father and Mother raised their hands.

"Well, there goes our holiday," Mother said.

Margaret hugged Mother. "It'll be fun. You'll see. Should I fetch my journal? I was keeping one as a pregnancy/holiday one. I can add the murder enquiry to it."

I grinned. "You wouldn't want the personal details about

your pregnancy to be combined with those of the investigation. You never know who'd be reading it."

"Um, you do have a point."

I was surprised Margaret had made that offer, as she was the wisest of us all. Maybe her pregnancy had something to do with it.

"I saw some really pretty journals in the hotel shop." Lady Mellie suggested. "Shall I fetch one?"

"Please do," Margaret said. "If you don't mind."

"Of course not." Lady Mellie wasted no time going in search of the journal.

"May I say something?" Mother asked.

"Of course."

"You will need privacy to conduct your discussions."

"And your suite will not do," I said, knowing where she was headed.

"It's fine for tonight, Kitty. I don't want to inconvenience anyone. But future meetings should be held in a business room. The hotel must have one you can use."

"There's the one where we talked to the Superintendent. It's small, but I think we can make do." I glanced at Robert. "The Brighton constabulary can be charged for the cost."

"The Superintendent will need to approve the expense," Robert said.

"It's the least he can do. After all, he's getting your services for free."

He called down to the lobby and asked to talk to the assistant manager. After Robert ended the call, he said, "He's assigning us a conference room for the investigation, larger than the one where we talked to Superintendent Merton. We can have it as long as we need. Compliments of the hotel. He's sending up the key."

"Excellent," I said.

Lady Mellie soon returned, breathless and pink-cheeked. "They had some gorgeous journals. I chose the prettiest one."

It was indeed beautiful with watercolor images of the Brighton shore, the pier, and of course, the Royal Pavilion on the cover. After she handed the journal to Margaret, Sebastian passed to my sister a writing instrument he retrieved from his jacket. Encased in 18K gold and black onyx with a gold and silver nib, the valuable fountain pen had been a birthday gift from Margaret.

As we arranged ourselves around the seating room. "Now, where were we?" I asked.

"You were asking Ned about Lady Litwell's finances," Margaret said.

Ned glanced at Father who nodded. "Lady Litwell inherited her fortune from her late husband, a partner in a diamond mine. Before he passed away, he set up a trust, naming Lady Litwell as his sole beneficiary. The trustee, the entity that manages the trust, is a London law firm. We make suggestions based on the amount we're allowed to invest. Once the trustee approves it, we invest the funds. As of the latest report we submitted to the law firm, we'd invested 100,000 pounds in various ways."

"Who's the subsequent beneficiary?" Marlowe asked. He might act the fool, but he had a sharp mind, especially when it came to finances.

"That was not something we needed to know," Ned responded. "But since we have a relationship with the law firm, I can make an enquiry."

"Please do," Robert said. "If they refuse to cooperate, let me know. I can ask Scotland Yard to step in."

"Will do."

A knock on the door interrupted our discussion.

As Robert was closest, he opened the door. A familiar face stood on the other side.

"Hollingsworth!" Robert said. "I thought you were in Bristol seeing to your ship."

"I was," Hollingsworth said stepping into the room. "They're doing a bang-up job, and I was just getting in the way. So, I thought I'd join you."

"Where's Lady Charlotte?" I asked. "You did not leave her behind?"

"She'll be along. She wanted to change clothes before she joined us."

If I knew Lady Charlotte, and I did, she'd also have a quick wash. Train travel can be awfully dusty. "And Lady Aurelia?"

"She opted to remain in London as she was looking forward to sleeping in her own bed."

Her bed being on the top floor of the Ladies of Distinction Detective Agency where her quarters were located. When Lady Emma and I had offered her the position of Assistant Lady Detective, we'd offered her the free use of the top floor as an incentive to come work for us. I doubted we could pry her out of the space with a crowbar, she loved it so much.

"You've arrived in time for cocktails," I said.

Hollingsworth smashed his palms together. "Oh, Ho, and a bottle of rum. Just what a sailor needs."

"What's your poison?" Ned asked approaching the drinks cart.

"Whiskey neat." Within a few seconds, he had a glass tumbler in his hand.

"Ahhh," Hollingsworth said after taking a sip. "So, are you enjoying your holiday?"

Lady Mellie snickered.

Hollingsworth's brow knitted. "What's so humorous, dear sister?"

She grinned. "There's been a murder."

70

He paused with the glass halfway to his mouth. "Another one? Blimey."

"Language, Lord Hollingsworth," Mother gently chided.

"My apologies, ma'am," he said with a quick bow.

"Kitty and Inspector Sinclair discovered the body in the beach hut Mister Worthington rented," Lady Mellie said.

"By Jove."

Another knock on the door which Robert answered once more. "Lady Charlotte, welcome!"

"To the madness!" I said raising my own glass.

She'd slipped into a fresh gown and appeared, indeed, to have taken a quick wash as her still wet, riotous red locks attested. But sea faring lass that she was, she wasn't one to mind such a thing.

"Thank you," she said a tad confused. I had no doubt she would catch up in no time.

"We need to alert the restaurant and change our reservation numbers," Mother said counting heads. "Thirteen? Oh, my, that's an unfortunate number."

"Maybe we could invite Lord Harrington," Marlowe said with a smirk. "Then our numbers would be even."

"That's not remotely humorous," Lady Emma hissed at him.

"My dear Lady Emma, it wasn't meant to be." There was a definite bite to his words.

So much for his couldn't-care-less attitude.

"We'll make do," Mother rushed to say, eager to pour oil over troubled waters.

Another knock on the door. Who could it be now? We were all here.

Robert once more attended to it. The policeman who'd been assigned to assist with the investigation, stood in the corridor.

"Constable Brown," Robert said.

"Sorry to interrupt, sir. But I wanted to report on the matter of the beach hut key."

"Please come in." Once the policeman stepped into the room, Robert asked. "What did you find?"

"Well, sir" —Constable Brown ran a finger under his collar— "During the last six months, only two keys were not returned. One was assigned to Lord Reginald Rollins. An elderly gentleman seemingly quite infirm. He'd traveled to Brighton to enjoy the sea air."

"Not a likely candidate to commit a murder."

"No, sir."

"And the other one?"

"Mister Grimes. A family of eight. Two parents and six children. Apparently, one of the children lost the key."

"Umm, that has possibilities." The keys were numbered and so were the beach huts. So if someone found it, they could easily determine which lock it would open.

"Yes, sir. They're a local family. They took rooms at The Majestic so they wouldn't have to travel back and forth from town."

Made sense. With six children to mind, it would have made life easier.

"I'd be glad to interview Mister and Mrs. Grimes and see if I can discover more details," Constable Brown volunteered.

"Splendid idea," Robert said. "We can discuss it in the morning."

"Yes, sir." Constable Brown turned to leave.

But before he could do so, Mother stopped him. "Pardon me, young man."

"Yes, ma'am."

"Have you had your supper?"

"No, ma'am. I was going to stop at the chippy before heading home."

"Chippy?" Mother was not familiar with that term.

"Fish and chips takeaway, ma'am."

"Well, we can do better than that. Would you care to join us for supper? We're headed for the hotel restaurant now."

"Me!" Constable Brown's voice squeaked as his eyes widened. "Thank you, ma'am, but I'm not really dressed for a fancy dinner."

"You're wearing your policeman's uniform. I can't think of anyone better dressed." When he tried to decline again, she stopped him. "I will suffer no arguments, young man. You're coming along with us."

CHAPTER 13

THE INVESTIGATIVE COMMITTEE MEETS

*A*fter breakfast the next morning, we gathered in the
Tidepool, the charmingly named conference room
the hotel had assigned to us. Painted in shades of blue and
green, with touches of beige, it recalled the beach itself which
aimed to provide a serene atmosphere. Whether it actually
achieved that goal was something to be determined. At times,
our discussions could become quite heated. I welcomed the
overhead electric fan. With so many of us in the space, the
room was bound to be warm. The hotel had kindly provided
pitchers of tea and fruit juices as well as a bucket of ice.

Except for Mother and Father, every one of our friends
and family were there, even Margaret. A good thing for no
one took notes as expertly as she did. Constable Brown was
not present as he had been dispatched to interview the
family who lost the key. He would provide his report at a
later time.

Before the meeting, Robert and I had decided on the

agenda. We would start with a summary of everything that had happened, including our interviews of Lord Litwell and his daughter, Lady Esther. Once we'd done so, we proceeded with the one item we'd discussed the night before.

"Ned, have you made plans to telephone the law firm?" Robert inquired.

"Already have. My contact was reluctant to discuss Lady Litwell's trust as he needed to consult the main partner. But he promised to call later today with an answer.

"If the law firm turns down your request—" Robert said.

"I'll let you know."

"When can we expect the postmortem?" Lady Emma asked.

"Later today, unless the medical examiner runs into complications," Robert answered.

"You talked with Lord Litwell and his daughter, but what about his son?" Lady Emma once more.

"He's out to sea, literally, on a sailing trip. Hopefully, he'll return this afternoon. I'll talk to him then."

"Was he in Brighton when Lady Litwell was killed?"

"That's to be determined. We'll know more when I interview him."

Lady Mellie raised her hand. "I think we should visit the scene of the crime."

"We don't want to trample any evidence, Lady Mellie."

"We wouldn't have to enter the beach hut. We can walk around it, examine it from the outside. See if we can find another way in."

"There isn't, I assure you," Robert said.

"I think it's a great idea, Robert," I said. "It can't hurt. We're the only ones who've been in the beach hut. They need to see it for themselves."

Robert did not appear too pleased. Still, he approved the

suggestion. "Fine. Wear your beach shoes." He grinned. "There's a lot of sand out there."

"Very funny," I said.

After we all changed into appropriate wear, we made our way en masse to the hut. It was locked, of course, but Robert had the key.

After he opened the door, he allowed everyone to peek into the space. There wasn't much to see. The beach hut consisted of four walls, one door, and one window. The walls were painted bright blue and red with green accents here and there. I pointed out the changing room, small table, and two chairs.

"It doesn't have a bathroom?" Lady Mellie asked.

"Afraid not," Robert answered. "Nor does it have running water. The reason this one is so popular is that it's close to the public restrooms and shower facilities." He pointed to them located twenty feet from where we stood.

"Maybe someone visiting the restrooms late that night saw something," Lady Emma suggested.

"In the dark?" Lord Marlowe scoffed. "I doubt anyone could see two feet in front of them."

"It could have happened," Lady Mellie said. "It was cloudy, but there was a full moon that night."

"I'll have Constable Brown make some enquiries." Robert said, effectively ending that discussion.

"Other than the strangulation marks on Lady Litwell's neck," Ned asked, "were there any other signs of violence on her?"

"None as far as I could see," Robert said. "Since I was not in charge of the investigation at the time, I hesitated to disturb the scene. But the medical examiner should have more information."

Although we spent another fifteen minutes or so walking around the beach hut and peering into it, we were not able to locate any clues. If any had existed in the first place, the wind and the sand would have done their damage. Still, the group continued to ask questions.

"Is the front door the only way someone can enter the bathing box?" Hollingsworth asked.

"Yes," Robert answered.

"What about the window?" Sebastian asked.

"It's too small for someone to slip through it, as you can see."

"So, what do you think happened?" Lady Charlotte asked of Robert.

"Lady Litwell met someone here around midnight. Reason to be determined. That person strangled her and then walked out locking the door behind him."

"You think it was a man?" Lady Charlotte asked.

"It takes a prodigious amount of strength to strangle a person. The marks around her neck were ones that only a man could make."

"Or a woman with large hands." As if to prove a point, she held up her own. Lady Charlotte was tall, almost Amazonian in stature. A woman of a similar built could have indeed committed the murder.

"Point taken, Lady Charlotte," Robert said. "I'll bear it in mind."

Lady Charlotte simply nodded. She wasn't the kind to belabor a point.

"We've seen all there is to see, so we should head back to the hotel," Robert said. "Ned is expecting a phone call from the law firm, and Constable Brown could've returned from his interview of the Grimes family. I also must report at two to the Brighton constabulary for the press conference. Other than the bare facts, neither the superintendent nor I will have much to share. But it's something that needs to be done."

Somewhat deflated, we returned to The Majestic where indeed there was a message for Ned. He needed to call the law firm as soon as possible. After agreeing we would meet again at four in the Tidepool room, we went our separate ways.

Robert had neither invited me, nor would I have accepted, an invitation to join him at the press conference. We'd drawn a bright line between his public duties as a Chief Detective Inspector at Scotland Yard and his less visible ones. Although he more than welcomed my participation in the investigation, it would not be proper for me to be seen next to him during the press conference. Both of us were happy with this mutually agreed-upon decision.

I stopped at one of the hotel shops to buy a new journal. Although I'd brought one to Brighton to memorialize our wonderful holiday, I needed a separate one for the investigation. After a bath and a change of clothes in my room, I set about writing my thoughts. It was my belief that no one had witnessed what happened that night. Even with a full moon, it would've been too cloudy for anyone to see anything. Still, I drew a quick sketch of the beach hut and the surrounding area. One never knew when it could be needed. An hour later, I was done.

Feeling like I needed to do more, I decided to visit Lady Esther. She was likely to open up more to a lady than a gentleman. Without further thought, I made my way to her room. Luckily, she was in, although she was not alone. Her brother, Oscar, had returned.

Clearly, he'd been out to sea. He was deeply tanned, and his tousled hair had been exposed to the salt of the ocean. The sun had had an effect on it as well since it had lightened somewhat since last I'd seen him.

After Esther introduced us, he wasted no time in getting to the heart of the thing. "So you're associated with the investigation into my stepmother's murder, Miss Worthington?"

"I am. My fiancé, Chief Detective Inspector Robert Crawford Sinclair is leading it, but I'm helping with the enquiries." I needed to be clear as to my role. I did not wish him to remotely entertain the wrong ideas.

"How very interesting," Oscar said with a sneer to his lips.

"Miss Worthington has her own detective agency, Oscar," Lady Esther said. "Don't you remember? We read about her in one of the London papers. She handled that murder investigation, the one associated with Andover I think."

"The Kingdom of Andover," I clarified.

"Oh, yes," Oscar said. "Somebody lost his head at the Tower of London. How very gruesome." He didn't sound horrified. Just the opposite, he seemed amused.

"Yes, it was horrific." As I was eager to focus on the current investigation, not a past one, I turned the conversation in another direction, "How may I address you, sir?" As the son of an earl, he had to have a courtesy title.

"Lord Devon is my courtesy title, but please call me Oscar."

He was trying to be charming. But it didn't impress me as I had seen the best. "I can't do that, Lord Devon. It wouldn't be proper. But thank you for the offer."

"Will you put the thumbscrews on me?" He smirked.

"I leave that to Robert. He's much better at it than I am." Clearly, it would do no good to talk to Esther with him present, so I asked her if she'd had her luncheon. When she replied she hadn't, I invited her to the Grotto, purposefully not including her brother in the invitation.

"I'll leave you to it then," Oscar said. "I need a wash before I talk to Father." He seemed to take the snub in stride. But then it would have been totally inappropriate for me to issue him an invitation. Surely, he knew that.

"Shall I bring my hat?" Lady Esther asked with a beaming smile. Clearly, she was excited about the prospect of the luncheon.

"You won't need one. I'm not wearing one, as you see."

"Stepmama always cautioned me to wear one in public."

Oscar's face scrunched with disapproval, whether it was directed toward his sister or his deceased stepmother was anybody's guess. "She's gone, Esther. You don't have to follow her strictures anymore."

The three of us made our way out of Lady Esther's room and down the corridor. His room apparently was located on another floor. But rather than ride the lift, he chose to take the stairs that rose all the way from the lobby. Clearly, he was fit, as he took them two at a time. Was he showing off or in a hurry to get away?

CHAPTER 14

A LUNCHEON AT THE GROTTO

"Thank you for inviting me," Esther said. "I don't often get an opportunity to enjoy time with another young lady."

"Don't you engage with them at balls and such?" I asked.

"I'm not out yet."

She was seventeen, I reminded myself. Although many young ladies were brought out at that age, she was not one of them.

"Were plans being made for your debut next season?" By March, she would be close to eighteen, if not that already.

"No. Not really." Her face flushed pink. "Papa is busy with his estate, and Stepmama is, er, did not wish to get involved in such an endeavor. Now, with her sad demise, that will be out of the question."

"I'm sorry for your loss."

"Thank you. She wasn't the pleasantest of individuals, but

her marriage to Papa allowed him to pay off the estate debts. Without the funds she settled on him, I don't know what would have happened to us." She glanced down at her hands as she stated, "I did admire her, you know."

"Did you really?" How very odd. If I were in her shoes, I certainly wouldn't have.

"She rose from poverty to make something of herself."

"Did she?" I asked hoping to learn more about her step-mother's background. It was the kind of information we needed to know to solve Lady Litwell's murder.

"Her father moved the family to South Africa to improve their fortune. Except there was no fortune to be had. After he died from working himself to death, the mother did what she could. But she succumbed to some disease. At a very young age, my stepmother was left parentless. Her one asset was her beauty."

"She was beautiful." In a cold, cruel kind of way.

"She apparently used it very effectively to attract the notice of her first husband."

I could imagine a way or two she could have done that. As rich as that gentleman was, she would have set her sights on marriage and employed whatever means necessary to make that happen.

"Within months of their meeting, he married her. She told me he was so enthralled, there was nothing he wouldn't do for her. Sadly, the marriage lasted but a few years. He died from the bite of a venomous snake."

"How did the marriage to your father come about?"

"She contacted a marriage broker in London who put Papa in touch with her. Marriage plans were made and agreed upon before she even left South Africa. A short time after her arrival in England, the wedding ceremony was held."

"Their marriage was amicable?"

Lady Esther shrugged. "They rubbed along well enough, I suppose. But she resented Papa paying more attention to his estate than her. During their first year of marriage, he did join her in London so she could enjoy the season. But afterward, he refused to do so claiming his properties needed all his attention."

"So, she braved the season alone?" She wouldn't be the first peeress to do so. Still, it would have created some awkwardness at invitations to suppers. Hostesses preferred even numbers at their tables.

"Oh, she'd made acquaintances by then. But she was never really accepted, not socially anyways. The lords and ladies tolerated her presence, but she wasn't invited to the more prestigious events."

"Because of her modest background?"

"That was my guess, although it could have easily been her . . . forceful personality."

Downright rude would be a better word, but would she have acted in such a manner in a social setting? She would have been a fool if she had. And Lady Litwell had not struck me as one. It was something that needed to be determined. For now, I needed to obtain more information. "She must have resented being shunned in such a manner."

"She did. She would storm back to our estate in the Cotswolds and rant and rave at Papa, as if it was his fault."

"Lord Litwell did not mind?"

"Oh, he took it all in stride. After such outbursts, she only remained a few days before returning to London. He knew he wouldn't have to put up with it for long."

"What did she do after the season ended?"

"She returned to our estate in August, and the following month she would host a huge gathering. She offered the finest foods, the best entertainment. Nothing was too much. Plenty of the nobility attended as they were eager to partake of her largesse. But at the end of the two weeks, they'd return to their own homes or move on to the next country party. She was never invited to those."

"And afterwards? Did she remain in your estate?"

"Only the first two years. After that, she traveled to Paris, Rome, Venice. She especially loved Venice. I think she met someone there last year. An artist would be my guess. She brought back many paintings with her. Utter rubbish in my opinion."

"Are you knowledgeable about art?"

"Not knowledgeable, exactly, but I do paint. When I go for walks, that's what I do."

"I would love to see your pieces. I love to sketch."

Esther beamed with happiness. "When we finish our luncheon, I can show them to you, if you wish.

"Marvelous." At least the poor thing had an outlet for her lonely existence.

The server arrived with our chosen fare, so we spent some time addressing our meals.

Once she satisfied her hunger, Lady Esther asked, "Is Inspector Crawford Sinclair attending to the investigation at the moment?"

"Yes. The superintendent of the Brighton Constabulary is holding a press conference this afternoon. Robert's presence was requested."

"Have you found anything of note?" she asked, a note of hesitation in her voice.

Of course, I could not share our progress with her. I could offer some hope, though. "It's early days. We're making enquiries." She couldn't possibly expect anything else. After all, we'd only discovered Lady Litwell's body yesterday.

"Do you often help your fiancé with his investigations?"

"Not really." Eager to get away from this topic, I asked, "Do you know any of Lady Litwell's acquaintances?"

"No. I rarely leave the Litwell estate."

"But Lady Litwell held house parties. Surely you met some then?"

"Oh, yes." Her face flushed pink. "I did not participate in them. In the past, I was too young. More recently, since I'm not out, it was deemed bad form. Also, I don't have the wardrobe to mingle with the nobility. I did occasionally run into some of the guests when I was painting at the Litwell Castle lake. But most pretty much ignored me."

Good heavens! I would need to have a word with her father after the investigation concluded. He had to do his duty and bring her out. Of course, with Lady Litwell's death, it couldn't be done for a year.

Once we finished our meal, Lady Esther expressed an interest in visiting one of the hotel shops. So, we wandered into one where we encountered Ladies Gloria and Meredith. They were admiring some locally crafted jewelry.

"Miss Worthington!" Lady Meredith said. "How very pleasant to see you."

I felt, more than saw, Lady Esther's reaction. She'd stiffened. How very odd.

Doing the polite thing, I performed the introductions.

Turned out, it was not necessary. "We've already met," Lady Meredith said with a pleasant smile. When Lady Esther didn't immediately respond, she prompted, "Last year? At the National Gallery? Harrington escorted me. Your brother, Lord Devon, was with you."

"Oh, yes." Lady Esther's brow cleared up. "I'd traveled to London to consult a physician. A minor ailment as it turned out. Dear Oscar, knowing how much I enjoy art, took me there."

"We heard about Lady Litwell," Lady Meredith said. "I'm so sorry. How very dreadful for you."

"Thank you. That is very kind of you to say so."

The bell over the door rang as a tall figure stepped into the shop. One I easily recognized. Lord Harrington, immaculately attired in a herringbone linen suit, blue shirt with a collar bar, and a yellow pocket square. A boater hat topped his luxuriant blond locks. To say he was a fashion plate was an understatement. But unlike Robert, whose elegant clothes were a natural part of him, Lord Harrington's attire seemed to have been chosen to impress more than anything else. He'd certainly achieved that, as he'd drawn the eye of every person in the shop.

"Oh, dear," Lady Esther said.

I turned back to her. She seemed flustered. Alarmed by her drastic change I asked, "Is something wrong?"

She brushed trembling fingers across her brow. "I'm feeling a bit faint. It's all been too much. I think I better return to my room."

"Of course. Here, lean on me," I said, putting my arm around her waist.

As we walked out, Lady Esther kept a distance from Lord Harrington. Something that was not hard to do as he'd spied his sister and Lady Gloria and was headed in their direction.

Upon reaching Lady Esther's room, we discovered her maid was missing. So I helped her out of her dress and into her robe. Although color had returned to her face, she was still shaky. So I offered the tried and true British comfort. "Shall I ring for some tea?"

"No. Thank you." She braved a smile. "But could you draw the curtains, please? The light is too much to bear."

Maybe she suffered from migraines. "Yes, of course."

After I did so, I said my goodbye as she clearly wanted solitude. Still, I wasn't about to totally desert her, so I promised to come back and check on her.

On the way to my room, I mulled over what had occurred. She'd been in a happy mood until Lady Meredith mentioned seeing her in London. And then she'd turned . . . wary? Why was that? She'd also had a visceral reaction to Lord Hollingsworth. Was it from fear? Or something else? Had something happened between them to cause her collapse? Whatever it was, I would have to find out.

CHAPTER 15

THE INVESTIGATIVE COMMITTEE MEETS (PART DEUX)

*L*ater that afternoon, the investigative committee reconvened. Not only were we eager to hear about the press conference but curious about Ned's report.

I didn't anticipate what Robert had to say, but, maybe in retrospect, I really should have. "Lady Litwell was drugged."

Gasps echoed around the room.

"That explains how she ended up at the beach hut," I said. "She was given something before she was taken there."

"That's my belief, yes," Robert said.

"Did the medical examiner identify the specific drug?" Lady Emma asked.

"A soporific."

"A sleeping draught?" Lady Lily exclaimed.

"There were packets on the night table next to her bed," I explained. "So, they'd be readily accessible."

"That would point to a family member," Lady Lily said.

"Or an acquaintance who knew she took sleeping powders," I said.

"But wouldn't her family have noticed someone entering her room?"

"I doubt it," I said. "Lady Litwell's suite was located on the opposite end of the corridor from her husband and step-daughter. Someone could have easily visited her without either of them being aware of it."

"Could have been a lover," Lady Charlotte suggested. "Her marriage was one of convenience, after all. And she was much younger than her husband. She probably had needs that weren't being satisfied."

Ladies Lily and Mellie met that statement with wide-eyed gazes. Probably curious to learn about these 'needs.'

"She had to have been carried to the bathing box, don't you think?" Lady Mellie asked. "After taking a sleeping draught, she would not have been able to make her own way."

"I don't see how," Robert said. "Someone would have noticed a body being hauled over a shoulder. That's the last thing the murderer would have wanted."

"Have any witnesses shown up at the constabulary?" Lord Hollingsworth asked.

"Not so far," Robert answered. "But then the press confer-ence was held only a couple of hours ago. It'll be in the late afternoon papers and tomorrow's early edition. Someone may very well come forward after that."

"How do you think she made it to the beach hut?" Sebas-tian asked.

"She could have been wobbly, but still able to walk, given the appearance of someone who'd imbibed a bit too much. Her murderer would have wrapped their arm around her to help her. Once they reached the privacy of the bathing box, killing her would have been an easy feat to accomplish."

"So either a family member or an acquaintance performed the deed."

"Although familiarity would certainly point to those individuals," I said, "it could have been someone else."

"Please explain," Robert said.

"Lady Esther mentioned her stepmother enjoyed a cup of tea before she went to bed at night. A hotel staff member could have brought it to her."

"Or someone disguised as a staff member," Lady Charlotte suggested. "Having slipped the sleeping draught into the cup, he or she could have easily waited for her to drink the tea and reentered her room at a later time."

Lady Emma huffed. "In other words, it could have been anyone."

"I'm afraid so," I said. "For the moment, let us put that topic aside and move on to Ned's report." It would be something concrete we could rely on, rather than the what ifs we were discussing.

Unfortunately, the report wasn't what we'd hoped for. "For the time being, the solicitor won't share any information." When I started to object, he said, "Wait. Hear me out."

As I had no choice, I nodded. "Go on."

"Normally, he waits until the day of the funeral to read the will. But given the nature of Lady Litwell's demise, the Brighton superintendent felt it best to do so as early as possible. So tomorrow, the solicitor is traveling to Brighton to read the will. It's scheduled for tomorrow at two. Once that is done, everything will be made clear. Or so he says."

"You will be present?" I asked.

"Yes. It's been arranged."

"All right. In the meantime, how shall we proceed?"

"Someone needs to talk to the hotel staff and find out if

Lady Litwell had food or drink delivered the night of her death," Lady Emma suggested.

"Have Sebastian do it," Margaret suggested. "They'll have a hard time saying no to a duke."

"Megs, are you sure?" Sebastian said, a look of concern on her face. Not hard to see where he was coming from. She was experiencing morning sickness, and he didn't want her to suffer alone.

"I'm feeling better, darling. No need to worry about me. While you're busy with those enquiries, I'll remain in our room organizing the case notes."

"Very well. If you're sure."

"Positive." She beamed him a smile. Clearly, the investigation was doing her a world of good.

"What would you like me to do?" Hollingsworth asked.

"I'm interviewing Lord Devon at five," Robert said. "I'd like you to come with me. Supposedly, he went sailing in the time surrounding Lady Litwell's death. Since you're a seaman, I'd like you to question him about it. What time did he set sail? When did he return? Where did he go? And then I'd like you to put the same questions to the boat owner."

"I'll be glad to," Lord Hollingsworth said.

"What about me?" Lady Emma asked.

"I'd like you to talk to Lady Meredith," I said.

"I barely know her," she rightfully pointed out.

"Seek out your sister. Engage with her. Chances are Lady Meredith won't be far. They seem to do everything together."

"All right. What do you want me to discuss with Lady Meredith?"

"Last year, Lady Esther traveled to London to consult a physician about a minor complaint. While she was in London, she ran into Lady Meredith at the National Gallery. When Lady Meredith brought it up today at the hotel shop, Lady Esther did not seem to recall that encounter. Not only that, she seemed wary. I want you to find out everything you can about that conversation. With any luck at all, Lady Esther mentioned the name of the physician. I have a feeling it's important."

"Consider it done," Lady Emma said.

"I assume you don't want me to accompany Lady Emma during her enquiry," Lord Marlowe said.

"No," I said. "I have a more important task for you. I want you to tell us about Lord Harrington."

He arched a brow. "No."

"Whatever you know about him, you must tell us," I insisted. After all, Lord Harrington had been invited to Lady Litwell's parties at Litwell Castle. So, he was known to her. "We need to learn the measure of the man."

"It has nothing to do with the present."

"How do you know it doesn't?" Lady Emma asked turning to him. "It could very well inform the investigation."

"Very well if you insist. But the younger ladies need to leave the room. The tale is not for their tender ears."

Ladies Lily and Mellie gazed at each other. After a silent communication passed between them, Lady Mellie said, "We're not leaving."

When Lord Marlowe remained silent, Lady Emma said, "Oh, for heaven's sake. They've been exposed to all kinds of horrors, Marlowe, including a decapitation. Speak!"

"It points to the depravity of the man."

"We understand," I said. "Now out with it. What did he do?"

"He seduced a young barmaid in Oxford, got her in the family way, and then abandoned her."

"And?" I prompted.

"That's it. Isn't that enough?"

"Is that why you got into a fight with him?" Lady Emma asked.

"I thought he'd try the same thing with you!"

"And you believed I'd be gullible enough to fall for his dubious charm?"

"You went off with him."

"To dance. I danced with him."

He crossed his arms across his chest as his mouth set in a mulish line. "That's how it starts, isn't it? With a dance."

"Marlowe," Lady Emma said in a soft voice. "I could never fall for him."

His mouth twisted. "Why not? He's rich, titled, not bad looking."

"Because it's you I love, you idiot!"

For a moment, there was dead silence in the room and then Marlowe got a silly grin on his face. "You love me?"

"I just said so, didn't I?" Lady Emma spit out in the least loverlike tone.

He frowned. "Then why won't you marry me?"

"You very well know why. I've told you enough times."

"But you wouldn't have to work as a lady detective! You'd be Lady Marlowe."

"It's not enough. Not for me. Why can't you see that?"

I cleared my throat. "Sorry to interrupt. But could the two of you leave the heart burnings for another time? Hopefully, when you can enjoy some privacy. We really do need to return to the matter at hand."

"Yes, of course," Lord Marlowe said. "My apologies." He got ahold of Lady Emma's hand, kissed it, and didn't let go. She didn't seem to mind. On the contrary, she appeared quite pleased.

"Now. Where were we?" I asked.

Margaret, of course, got us back on track. "Robert and Hollingsworth will interview Lord Devon at five. Sebastian will talk to hotel staff tomorrow morning, and Lady Emma will track down Lady Meredith."

"Succinct as always, dear sister. Thank you. That's all I have on my list. Robert? Do you have anything else?" I asked turning to him.

"Not at the moment."

"Let's adjourn then. We'll meet again tomorrow at four." That would give everyone enough time to perform their tasks. Hopefully, we'd have more information by then.

CHAPTER 16

A CLUE EMERGES

*L*ady Emma's task turned out to be easier than we thought. That evening during supper, Ladies Gloria and Meredith along with Lady Harrington visited our table to discuss their activities. While doing so, Lady Harrington expressed a desire to visit the Royal Pavilion. Unfortunately, she hadn't been able to explore it.

Lady Emma, seeing a golden opportunity when she saw it, declared herself equally fascinated and suggested they head there in the morning.

"I would love to do so," Lady Harrington said. "But I don't know if it can be accomplished as Harrington is not with us. Last night he received an urgent message which required him to travel to London for a day."

"I'll be glad to escort you, ma'am," Lord Marlowe said. "I've been curious to see it myself." A blatant lie for he thought the pavilion was an architectural abomination. But since he'd get to spend the morning with his lady love, he was all for it.

"Oh, how wonderful," Lady Harrington said. "It won't be an imposition?" Obviously, Lady Harrington was ignorant of the altercation between Marlowe and her son.

"It will be my pleasure, ma'am." He even tossed in an elegant bow, smooth operator that he was.

AFTER BREAKFAST THE NEXT DAY, Robert was expecting a telephone call from Scotland Yard. Of necessity, he needed to stay in his room. I wandered to Lady Esther's room to see if she wished to go for a walk along the shore. Thankfully, she was not only willing but eager to do so. Before we left, she showed me two of the sketches she'd drawn of the beach.

I was truly impressed. "You have real talent, Lady Esther. Your use of color is excellent. They very much resemble the school of expressionism."

Her cheeks turned rosy. "You think so?"

"Absolutely. Have you had a drawing instructor?"

"No. I'm self-taught."

"Maybe now there will be an opportunity to do so."

"What do you mean?"

"Well, your family might be mentioned in Lady Litwell's will. You might even find yourself the beneficiary of a small inheritance with sufficient funds to hire an instructor."

"That would be lovely!"

Hoping to learn more about her London visit, I asked, "I imagine you enjoyed your visit to the National Gallery. You can learn a great deal from its collections, especially the works of Monet and Renoir."

As before, she turned wary. "Yes. I did."

I threaded my arm through her elbow in a show of

friendship. "Forgive me for asking, but you seem uncomfortable discussing the topic of your visit to London last year. Does it have something to with your consult with a physician?" Intrusive, to say the least, but I needed to know her reason.

She turned her face away, probably unwilling to discuss the subject. But after a few moments, she met my gaze again. "It was a female complaint. My courses were two months' late. So Stepmama insisted we visit a London doctor. As it turned out, I had nothing to worry about."

"Ahhh, that's good to hear." Eager to smooth over the uncomfortable moment, I asked, "Shall we walk to that cove? It does appear quite inviting."

"If you don't mind, I'd prefer to return to the hotel."

"Yes, of course." Lady Esther was fragile to say the least. Knowing what I now knew about Lord Harrington, I had to wonder if he'd taken advantage of her while he was a guest at the Litwell estate. After saying goodbye to her, I headed toward Margaret's room. Hopefully, she was not suffering from morning sickness.

She seemed well enough when she opened the door. Still, I had to ask, "How are you faring?"

When she narrowed her gaze at me, I apologized. "Sorry, force of habit." Much like Mother, she hated to be asked about the state of her health. "It won't happen again."

She threw the door open wide. "Then you may enter, dear sister."

"Thank you, beloved," I said skipping into the room.

"Now that the pleasantries have been exchanged, what can I do for you?"

"Can't I just enjoy a visit with my sister without needing something?"

"Not when you're in the middle of an investigation, you can't. You always want something."

She knew me so well. "You are right. I do."

But before I could make my enquiry, we were interrupted by a knock on the door. "That must be the tea and toast I ordered."

"Queasy stomach?"

"In the mornings. In the afternoons, I could eat the proverbial horse."

Once the hotel employee departed, she asked, "So what did you wish to discuss?"

"Lady Esther and I went for a walk along the shore."

"During which time, you asked her about her London visit."

I grinned. "Along with your many talents, you've now become a mind reader."

"Umm," she said nibbling her toast. "What did you find out?"

"She visited the London doctor because her time of the month was late."

"How late?"

"Two months. Somehow, Lady Litwell found out, and she insisted her stepdaughter be examined by a London doctor."

"You would think a local one would have done," Margaret stated.

"My thoughts exactly. My guess is they didn't want anyone around the Litwell estate to know about the consult. Does the visit to the doctor mean what I think it means?"

"That Lady Esther could have been increasing?" Margaret asked. "A plausible explanation, to be sure."

"If in fact that was the case, it would have caused a great big scandal. Given Lady Litwell's social climbing ambitions, it was something she would have wished to avoid."

"Which explains why she whisked her stepdaughter to London. If she'd indeed been with child, she would have arranged for Lady Esther to take a trip abroad. Once she had the child, it would have been put in care, and Lady Esther would have returned to England with no one the wiser."

"Yes," I said, "I could very well imagine that happening."

"When did the visit to London happen?" Margaret asked.

"In November. That would have been roughly two months after Lady Litwell held a party at her estate. Could Lord Harrington have seduced Lady Esther?"

"It's certainly a possibility," Margaret said.

I shuddered. "Poor girl. But would that sequence of events have anything to do with Lady Litwell's murder?"

Her brow wrinkled. "What do you mean?"

"Could Lord Harrington have killed Lady Litwell?"

"That's a huge leap to make, Kitty. Why would he do that?"

"Because he seduced Lady Esther, and she threatened to reveal it?"

"We don't know that he seduced her. This is all guess-work on your part." She sipped her tea and nibbled more toast as she pondered the matter. "Lady Litwell supposedly took her stepdaughter to London to avoid a scandal. If she revealed Harrington seduced Lady Esther it would most certainly cause one. Why would she risk such a thing now?"

"Because another young lady might be in peril."

The penny dropped. "Good heavens! Lady Gloria?"

I nodded.

"You don't think he'd try to seduce her? Right under his mother's nose?"

"I doubt she'd notice. She's not in the best of health. And she didn't seem to know about the altercation between Harrington and Marlowe. If she did, she would not have agreed to Marlowe escorting them to the Pavilion."

"We need to warn Lady Emma."

"You're right." I glanced at my watch. "Drats. They're probably still on their visit to the Pavilion. They won't return until early afternoon as they were planning a luncheon in town as well."

"Well, at least Lord Harrington is out of town. Time enough to think things through. Tread carefully, Kitty. You're making conclusions based on suppositions. You'll need to find out if there is a factual basis for them."

Another thought occurred to me. "If Lord Harrington has tried anything with Lady Gloria, Marlowe will beat him to a pulp."

"If Sebastian, Robert, and Ned don't get to him first."

I bid her goodbye and headed to Robert's room to discuss this latest development.

CHAPTER 17

A DISCUSSION WITH ROBERT

*W*hen Robert opened the door, I did not give him the chance to offer anything more than a greeting.

"Are you done with your telephone call?" I asked stepping into his room.

"Yes. What's wrong?" He closed the door behind me.

I shared the conversation I had with Esther and the conclusions I'd reached.

"You believe Harrington seduced Lady Esther and supposedly got her pregnant. When Lady Litwell found out Lady Esther's courses were late, she took her to London so a physician could examine her. But it turned out she wasn't. Is that correct?"

"Yes."

He let out a sigh as his kind gaze found me. "She did not say she'd been carrying a child, Catherine."

"It's a logical conclusion that could be drawn."

His brow arched. "Did it ever occur to you that Lady Esther could be lying?"

"Why would she do that?"

"It could have been Lady Litwell who visited the physician. Maybe she was the one who thought she was increasing."

"And she used Lady Esther as a beard?"

"Yes."

"But why would it matter to her? Lady Litwell was a married woman."

Taking my hand, he guided me to the small sofa in his room before settling next to me. "Darling, Lady Litwell did not enjoy relations with her husband. If she was with child, it would not have been his. Lady Esther herself told you her stepmother traveled extensively. What if she took a lover while visiting one of those foreign cities and got pregnant. She would have wanted to take measures to prevent a child being born."

"But Lady Litwell did not have a child. We would have heard about it."

"Exactly. There are ways of getting rid of an unwanted pregnancy, Catherine."

"She wouldn't have done that!"

"Oh, wouldn't she? The more I find about the lady, the less I want to investigate her murder."

"Balderdash! We both know you're too honorable and committed to duty to stop."

"Yes, well, there is that," he said with a grin.

"I gather you discovered something about Lady Litwell during your telephone call."

"I did. Her first husband's death was rather suspicious. He died from the bite of a venomous snake, one that had mysteriously made its way into his bed. No one knew how it ended up where it did."

"You think she put it there?"

"There were rumors, but nothing could be proven. Apparently, she was visiting a sick friend quite a distance away when her husband died."

"Why would she kill her husband? He apparently treated her like a queen."

Capturing my hand, he brushed a thumb along the surface of my palm, a loving caress he often employed. "Like Lord Litwell, he was much older than her. Apparently, she had quite a reputation before she married. She liked men, and men liked her. His death would've made her a rich widow, one who could indulge her carnal appetites."

"Lady Esther said she traveled to distant places after her country parties ended. Last year, her stepmother went to Venice. Lady Esther thought she'd taken a lover. An artist apparently because her stepmother returned with many paintings. Atrocious ones according to her." I sighed. "I jumped to a conclusion without enough facts. Not very professional of me."

He cupped his hand on my cheek. "We'll get there."

"I hope so." Shaking off my frustration, I asked, "How was your interview with Oscar?" Although he'd talked to him the day before, we hadn't had a chance to discuss it.

"He set sail the previous evening. In other words, he wouldn't have been in Brighton at the time Lady Litwell was murdered. Hollingsworth will be verifying that information with the man who owns the boat. Apparently, he rents it but takes it out himself. He doesn't trust anyone else to do so."

"But why take a boat out at night?"

"He wanted to see the stars over the ocean."

I wrinkled my nose. "The man does not strike me as a lover of nature. He's a gambler. The only reason I can think of is that there's money in it."

"Or maybe something else."

"Such as?"

"Scotland Yard shared some news about him."

"Why?"

"I'd requested information, not only about Lady Litwell, but the entire family. They didn't have anything on Lady Esther. Lord Litwell is seen as a retiring aristocrat totally involved with his estate. But they did have a file on Oscar."

"What did it contain?"

"Last year, at a private ballroom in Holland Park Avenue, sixty men were arrested in a police raid. Undercover officers had witnessed them dancing, kissing, and . . . performing other acts while wearing makeup and women's clothes. Lord Devon was one of the men."

"He prefers men?" He hadn't struck me as a homosexual, but then, what did I know?

"Apparently. He avoided prosecution because he was not one of the ones performing, er,—"

"Other acts."

"Yes."

"Well, I never."

"Yes."

"Such a thing is illegal, I gather."

"Very much so. Especially when done in public."

"But why?"

"There are laws against such conduct."

"Even when they're performed among consenting adults?"

"Yes."

"Well, the laws are wrong." After thinking about it for a moment, I asked, "Have you ever been involved in such raids?"

"No. I do not handle such matters."

"Well, thank heavens for that."

"What's happening with the inquest?"

"Superintendent Merton is holding off on it."

"Don't tell me. The coroner is on holiday."

He grinned. "The lady gets it in one."

"Unbelievable."

"Now, my darling Catherine, shall we go enjoy a luncheon at the Grotto? My stomach is in dire need of food."

"Yes, please." We had to snatch whatever bits of normalcy we could in the middle of this nightmare.

CHAPTER 18

THIRD MEETING OF THE INVESTIGATIVE
COMMITTEE

*S*o much had happened between yesterday and today, Robert and I needed to draft an agenda of the order of things. I asked Ned to report first.

"What did the solicitor reveal about the will?"

"Lady Litwell left the bulk of her fortune to Lord Litwell, her reason being he's an honorable gentleman who keeps his promises. He'll be a wealthy man. Surprisingly, she dowered Lady Esther with 50,000 pounds to be placed in a trust until she turns twenty-five or marries."

"At which time the money will go into her husband's keeping, I imagine," Lady Emma said.

"Actually, the funds will remain in the trust to be used for 'necessary items as Lady Esther sees fit.'"

"That's unusual."

"Lady Litwell probably wanted her stepdaughter to have some say about her life," I said. "If a husband proved difficult,

106

she could withhold any funds until he behaved more appropriately."

"This mythical husband could have taken his frustrations out on her," Ned said. "We've seen that already."

"Yes." Dear Lady Wakefield whose husband regularly abused her for not giving him an heir. She'd lived through that ordeal and was now happily married to Lord Newcastle, a dear friend of ours. Together with their daughter, Lavender Rose, they were now thoroughly enjoying their lives.

Ned glanced at his notes once more. "Lady Litwell included a clause in the will. If anything happens to Lady Esther, her inheritance will be donated to a worthy cause."

"Which one?" I asked.

"An orphanage in South Africa. Apparently, after her parents died, Lady Litwell spent some time there. She also set aside some funds for the improvement of Lady Esther which includes a new wardrobe and finishing school fees so her stepdaughter could be polished before entering a marriage."

"Goodness. She thought of everything," Lady Lily said.

"When was the will drawn up?" I asked. "Did the solicitor say?"

"The original document was drafted at the time of her marriage to Lord Litwell. But it was substantially revised eight months ago."

I couldn't know which items were added to the will. But I strongly suspected it was the ones dealing with Lady Esther. If my suspicions were true, after their trip to London, Lady Litwell must have realized Lady Esther's chances of marrying a peer was in peril. Titled gentlemen required a wife who was pure. Maybe Lady Litwell sought to encourage marriage proposals with a substantial dowry. But it did beg the question. Why would Lady Litwell care?

As if she could read my thoughts, Lady Mellie asked,

"Why didn't Lady Litwell act on those things while she was alive?"

"Maybe Lady Litwell would have spent the next few months doing just that. Lady Esther is only seventeen." Eager to move the discussion away from Lady Esther, I asked Ned, "What about the stepson?"

"She left him 10,000 pounds which she's sure he'll squander in a year."

"Obviously, she had no trust in him," Marlowe said.

"Anything else, Ned?" I asked.

"No."

"Thank you for your report. Let's move along to Robert, shall we?"

"I interviewed Oscar yesterday. Two days ago, he went sailing in the evening and didn't return until early afternoon the following day. So, he was not here during the time of the murder."

"What was he doing at night on a boat?" Lady Lily asked. "That's a rather odd time to go sailing."

"He wanted to see the stars over the ocean," Robert responded. "Or so he said."

"But you don't believe him," Lady Mellie said.

"Let's just say, I don't believe that was his only reason." And then he punted, "Hollingsworth may be able to shed some light on that matter. He talked to the owner of the sailboat."

As an officer of the law, he was unable to broach the subject of Oscar's sexual preference. So, he'd turned over that responsibility to his best friend.

They must have discussed it, because Hollingsworth readily shared what he'd discovered. "Lord Devon went on board with a companion."

"Who?" Marlowe asked.

"Another gentleman. They spent most of their evening

below deck, inside the cabin. They emerged at night to 'gaze at the stars' much as Robert has reported. According to the boat owner, they were both quite drunk. They'd brought with them a basket of food and several bottles of spirits."

Lady Lily frowned. "What on earth were they doing below deck for that many hours?"

The gentlemen all gazed at each other. Lady Emma raised a brow. Lady Charlotte put on a stone face. No one said a word.

Except for Robert, that is, who said, "I suppose we'll never know."

We may not have 'known,' but we all suspected. Except for Ladies Lily and Mellie, that is. They were too innocent to know the ways of some men.

"So he was definitely not in Brighton when Lady Litwell was murdered," Ned said.

"No, he was not. That's been confirmed."

"That leaves Lord Litwell."

"He must be ruled out as well as he was in his room at that time," Sebastian said.

"How do you know that?" Margaret asked.

"I spoke to the hotel staff. There was a delivery of tea to Lady Litwell's room. The same person delivered another tea tray, as well as liver scraps, to Lord Litwell's room."

"Liver? At midnight? The kitchen would have been closed."

"He'd requested the service earlier apparently. The liver was for the dog. Apparently, he couldn't sleep unless he had a treat."

"She," I clarified. "Miranda is the dog's name."

"He still could have murdered Lady Litwell," Ned insisted.

"How?" Sebastian countered. "The dog would have barked her head off if she'd been left alone. No. I don't think he did it."

"Was Lord Litwell aware he would benefit in the will?" Lady Charlotte asked. "That would provide him with a great motive."

"The solicitor said Lady Litwell wished for the terms to be kept confidential. She specifically mentioned it at the time the will was drawn and when it was revised."

"Well, that rules him out," Lady Emma said. "Which means we have no suspects."

"We're not done yet," I said. "Robert why don't you continue with your report."

"I asked Scotland Yard to investigate the family. Lord Litwell is exactly what he appears to be. An honorable gentleman with no skeletons in his closet. His former wife, Lady Esther's mother, suffered from melancholia. She was admitted to a sanatorium and died quite young. They don't know anything about Lady Esther. Oscar, however, does have a file, but I've determined it has no bearing on the investigation as he was out to sea."

"What was in it?" Lady Mellie asked.

"I prefer not to discuss it. It's a rather delicate subject."

I nodded. "You'll have to trust Robert, Lady Mellie."

"Maybe Oscar didn't do it," Lady Mellie said, "but he could have arranged for someone to kill his stepmother."

"There's no indication such was the case," Robert said. "He's apparently low on funds at the moment, and he didn't know he would stand to inherit 10,000 pounds."

"Well, somebody murdered Lady Litwell," Lady Mellie said. "She didn't strangle herself. Did she have any enemies? Someone from her past maybe?"

"All great questions that bearing looking into," I said. "But let's move on. Lady Emma what did you find out?"

"Not much. Lady Esther did not provide any information about her doctor's visit other than what Lady Esther said."

"A minor complaint?"

"Yes."

Lady Emma brightened up. "However, my conversation with Lady Harrington was quite illuminating."

"What did she say?"

"Apparently, she's been pressuring Harrington to marry. As frail as she is, she's afraid she will never see him wed. She's grown quite concerned about his lack of interest in the married state."

"How old is he?" I asked.

"In his early thirties, same as me," Marlowe responded. "Of course, he's not interested in marriage. He'd rather play the rake. We know what he did to that barmaid."

"About that," Robert said. "I put in a call to Inspector Bolton at Oxford and asked him to investigate it. Apparently, it caused quite an uproar about ten years ago."

"That's about right," Marlowe said.

"You didn't mention it when I talked to you earlier," I said.

"He called me back after you left, Catherine. Harrington was almost sent down. The scandal was that big."

"Why?" I asked.

"The barmaid visited the constabulary with a complaint. Apparently, she'd demanded compensation from Harrington, but he'd refused to give it. The superintendent refused to handle the matter and passed it on to the university. Somehow word leaked out, and all of Oxford found out. But then the barmaid moved away, presumably to have her child, and the whole thing died down. Months later, the barmaid returned to Oxford, sans child."

"She must have put it in care or given it to a family member to raise," Lady Emma suggested.

"The thing of it was," Robert said, "she returned with enough funds to set up her own pub. A quite successful one apparently. Bloom's."

"So, Lord Harrington must have paid her after all," I said.

"Apparently."

Ned cleared his throat. "May I add something?"

"Of course," I said.

"I heard of the pub while I was at Oxford. Bloom's contained a room which the owner rented for private meetings. The Rose and Thistle Club met there every Thursday evening. It was a gathering of like-minded fellows. Supposedly, they discussed intellectual topics of the day, but in reality, they planned rather disgraceful things."

Robert held up his hand. "We're bordering on a topic I'd rather not discuss at the moment."

"Why not?" Lady Mellie asked.

"If it is what I think it is, I'll need to verify it with the Oxford constabulary and Scotland Yard. We'll table this discussion for now."

"Please excuse us for a moment," I said to the group before pulling my fiancé aside and speaking softly to him. "It tracks with my own conclusions. I think we should discuss it."

"It's all conjecture at this point, Catherine. A man's reputation is at stake. Never mind a lady's."

"From what Ned and Marlowe said, he can't have much of one. The lady's, of course, is another matter. Everyone will understand the need for discretion."

"It's Lady Esther, isn't it?" Lady Mellie's voice reached us. "Did Lord Harrington steal her virtue?"

I gazed at Robert. "See! They realize it already."

"Very well," Robert nodded to me before turning back to the group. "But please keep in mind, we have no proof."

"We have proof about what he did to the barmaid," Lord Marlowe reminded him.

"The tales about the Rose & Thistle Club are true," Ned said. "I heard it from several sources."

"Which they could have learned from one another," Robert said.

"I know how to differentiate between a rumor and fact, Robert."

Ned had a point. During the Great War, he'd worked for the War Department. We never knew what he did. The Official Secrets Act prohibited him from discussing it. But I could very well imagine he dealt with information gathering. So, yes, he'd be able to tell rumor from fact.

"We will discuss these topics," Robert said, "but until we can verify them, we can't take them as facts. Is that understood?"

Everyone nodded.

"Catherine, explain your theory." I explained the conclusion I'd drawn from the conversations I'd had with Lady Esther and her reaction to Lord Harrington.

"I follow your reasoning, Kitty," Lady Emma said. "But how does it all lead to Lady Litwell's murder?"

"I think Lady Litwell was demanding Lord Harrington marry her stepdaughter."

"Why would she do that?"

"She's a social climber. The Harrington title has been around almost since the time of the conquest. Maybe she thought if Harrington married Lady Esther she would gain access to the higher strata of society, and she wouldn't be shunned anymore."

"But Harrington would have never agreed to such a marriage. His own mother said he has no desire to wed."

"He seemed interested in Lady Emma," Lady Lily pointed out.

"He knew it wouldn't lead anywhere," Lady Emma said. "It's my belief he did it in front of his mother to placate her." She gazed at me. "You believe Lady Litwell had some way to force him into marriage?"

"I do. But before I explain my reasoning, let us hear from Ned about the Rose & Thistle Club. What exactly do they do?"

"Once a month, they hold rituals in secret locations. Dressed as clergy, they mock the church, imbibing sacramental wines while enjoying relations with women dressed as nuns."

"Heavens!" I said. "And the club is still in operation?"

"I believe so. The locations of the rituals are sent to the members a bare hour before it occurs. Every member is thoroughly vetted before he is admitted to the club."

"Thank you, Ned. I believe Lady Litwell discovered Harrington's participation in these rituals and threatened to expose him unless he married Lady Esther."

"So, he killed her to stop her blackmailing him?"

"But why would he do that? He could have simply married Lady Esther and given Lady Litwell what she desired," Lady Lily said.

"Lady Litwell was the kind of woman that would have never stopped asking. Sooner or later, she would have demanded something else and more after that. She would have never been satisfied. By killing her, he silenced her permanently."

"How will we ever prove it? He'll never admit to it."

"I have an idea," Lady Mellie said.

CHAPTER 19

A PLAN IS SUGGESTED

"*L*et's hear it," I said.

"I'll suggest we take a stroll on the beach," Lady Mellie said.

"What makes you think he'll agree to do so?" I asked.

"I'll ask him in front of his mother. She likes me. And more than that, she sees me as an eligible wife for her son. I can phrase it in such a way she won't suspect any ulterior motives. Once we're alone, I'll tell him I saw him the night of the murder."

"You didn't, did you?" I asked.

"No. But he doesn't know that."

"How will you account for spotting him?"

"I couldn't sleep that night. Being away from home, I missed playing so I slipped down to the hotel lounge to play the grand piano that's there. The lounge has a massive window through which one can see the beach and the huts. For half an hour or so, I played several pieces, including *Clair de Lune* and *Moonlight Sonata*. They seemed appropriate for the place and time."

"The moon could not have been seen that night," I pointed out.

"Actually, it slipped in and out of the clouds."

"You would only have seen him if the time coincided with when he took Lady Litwell to the beach hut," Hollingsworth said. "You don't know when that happened."

"What time did you arrive at the lounge?" Robert asked.

"A few minutes before midnight," Lady Mellie answered.

Hollingsworth jumped to his feet. "Whatever you're thinking of doing, Mellie, I forbid it." Made sense he'd object. He was her brother after all.

"Why don't we see what she has to say?" Robert responded. "If the plan is too risky, we'll reject it. Please proceed, Lady Mellie."

She took a deep breath. "I'll then share with him everything we've discovered."

Loud objections echoed through the room. They all amounted to "You can't do that."

Lady Mellie took them all in stride. "It's no secret we're investigating Lady Litwell's murder. He knows we're all involved. He'll think I'm trying to trick him into confessing, especially when I tell him we're viewing him as our main suspect."

"What do you expect him to say?" I asked.

"More than likely, he'll deny I saw him. It's only my word against his, after all. He'll more than likely start to walk away. That's when I'll administer the coup de grâce."

"Which is?"

"His involvement with the Rose and Thistle Club. That's bound to get his attention. Ten years ago, he paid off that barmaid to save his reputation. He's the Earl of Harrington now. It's even more important to keep his licentious behavior from being known."

"All of us know about it," Ned said.

"But none of us are going to breathe a word. At least not in public. It would kill his mother and ruin his sister's chances of making an advantageous marriage. He'd know that."

"You're right," I said. "He'll probably bring up that reasoning."

"That's when I'll explain I'm in desperate straits. I need to marry quickly."

"Why?"

"As it happens, I was rather indiscrete with a footman and find myself in the family way."

"What?" Hollingsworth jumped to his feet. Again. Honestly, he was beginning to resemble a jack-in-the-box.

"Oh, for heaven's sake, Ollie," Lady Mellie said. "Of course, I did no such thing. But Lord Harrington would not know that."

Eager to keep the group's focus on her proposal, I asked, "Why would he believe you?"

"He'd know about the understanding I had with the Duke of Andover and the subsequent ending of that arrangement. I was so distraught I sought comfort in the arms of a footman."

"What would you demand of Harrington?" Lady Emma asked.

"A quick wedding given my circumstances. That's what I'd require in exchange for my silence."

"Even if he agreed to all this, it wouldn't help," I pointed out. "He still would not confess to the murder."

"You're right. He won't. I imagine he'll try to kill me instead."

"Are you insane?" Hollingsworth was so overwrought, he

actually grabbed her shoulders. Probably would have shaken them if she hadn't shrugged off his hold.

"No, dear brother," Lady Mellie calmly answered.

"Then why are you doing this?"

"I hate for that evil dastard to get away with murder. "You'll save me, Ollie. I know you will. And so will the rest of you. Inspector Crawford Sinclair can use that as leverage to get him to confess."

We spent the next hour arguing about it. In the end, we voted against her plan.

To say the least, Hollingsworth was visibly relieved.

Lady Mellie, however, was crestfallen. "It would have worked, you know," she said to the group.

"It's too dangerous, dear," I said. "There's no way we could control his actions."

"When does the bastard return from London?" Hollingsworth asked through gritted teeth.

If Mother had been present, she would have chastised him for his language. But she wasn't. And no one present dared do so. Not in the mood he was in.

I glanced at my wristwatch. "I imagine he's back by now." It was close to six. "Since cocktails will be in an hour, why don't we adjourn for the day? We'll reconvene tomorrow morning at ten."

CHAPTER 20

THE MORNING AFTER

*T*he following morning, a rather subdued group gathered in the restaurant for breakfast. Although we'd deemed Lord Harrington a strong suspect, we couldn't brand him as the murderer. We would need further evidence for that. But Robert had talked with both Scotland Yard and the detective inspector from Oxford. So hopefully, he would have some information to share.

Toward the end of our meal, Lady Mellie asked, "Do you mind if I don't participate in the committee meeting this morning?"

"Of course not," I said. "Participation is strictly voluntary."

"What will you do with your time?" Hollingsworth asked, sounding a bit suspicious.

"I thought to visit the hotel shops and buy some souvenirs as well as presents for the Worthington Manor staff. They have been very kind to me."

"It doesn't take two hours to shop for a few trinkets." The

usual length of our meetings.

"That's because you're not a lady." When he looked doubtful, she said, "Honestly, Ollie, there's no need to worry."

"Very well." But he didn't appear entirely convinced.

At our meeting, Robert shared the information he'd learned. Indeed, the Oxford inspector was indeed familiar with the Rose and Thistle Club. He confirmed ten years before or so, they'd held meetings at the pub. At the time, there'd been a great deal of talk, but nothing that could be verified. They'd never discovered the locations of their rituals. After their members graduated from Oxford, the club ceased to exist, at least in Oxford. London, however, was another story. According to Scotland Yard, the members had resumed their operations in and around the city. But much as Oxford, they'd never been able to discover the sites of their secret ceremonies. So, the group had largely gone unchecked.

The forensic department of the Brighton Constabulary had gathered fingerprints at the beach hut. They'd found hundreds which was only to be expected as that property was regularly rented out. Constable Brown would take the fingerprints of the Litwell family. I doubted they would match. But, of course, it was something that needed to be done. As far as Lord Harrington was concerned, there was no reason to get his, as we hadn't found a scintilla of evidence to connect him to the murder. Besides, if he had indeed strangled Lady Litwell, he would have been wise enough to wear gloves.

As we all needed a break, the meeting broke up around noon. Robert and I planned to take another walk to the pier before enjoying a late luncheon. The others had plans to head out as well. All of it came to a screeching stop in the lobby when we spotted Lady Mellie coming through the hotel's front door in the company of Lord Harrington.

"Bloody hell," Hollingsworth exclaimed as he rushed forward more than likely intent on doing some damage to the earl.

But before he could get anywhere near the earl, Robert stepped in front of him. "You don't want to do this."

"Yes, I do. Get out of my way."

Unfortunately, we were drawing the eye of every person in the space.

"If you hit him, it will cause a scandal, and your sister will be the one who suffers. You need to calm down."

For a few moments, his furious gaze bounced between Lord Hollingsworth, his sister, and Robert. Slowly, but surely, he regained control of himself. "If he's hurt her in any way—"

I glanced at Lady Mellie. She didn't appear upset. Just the contrary, she was smiling. "He didn't. Just look at her." I held up my hands. "Let me handle it."

"Fine," he said, stepping back.

"Lady Mellie," I said approaching her. "How fortuitous to run into you. I spotted the sweetest music box in one of the shops. A perfect one for your collection." I glanced back at Robert. "Didn't I say so, darling?"

"You certainly did, sweetheart."

"There, you see. I wanted to buy it for your birthday, but Robert said I should make sure you don't already have it."

"I don't know," Lady Mellie said. "I'd have to see it."

I curled my arm around her elbow. "Shall we go then? I'm anxious to buy it before somebody snaps it up." For the first time, I glanced at Lord Harrington. "I hope I'm not stealing her away."

"Most assuredly, you're not. We took a walk to the pier with my sister and Lady Gloria." He turned back to the two who'd just entered the hotel. "And here they are."

"We had the merriest of times, didn't we Gloria?" Lady

Meredith asked, joining her brother.

"We certainly did, Merry," Lady Gloria said, sliding next to her friend. "We stuffed ourselves silly, so much so I now need a nap."

Indeed, it appeared so, as their cheeks were rose-tinted, and their coiffures were windblown.

In the exchange of greetings, I separated Lady Mellie from the group. "Shall we head to the shop?"

"Yes, of course." But she wouldn't leave without saying goodbye to both young ladies and Lord Harrington. "Thank you for including me in your excursion."

Harrington bowed over her hand. "My pleasure, Lady Melissande. Until next time."

Although Lady Mellie nodded, she did not agree with him. As she and I walked away, Hollingsworth made a move toward Lord Harrington, but Robert easily stopped him again.

Rather than head to the shops, I guided Lady Mellie toward one of the lifts. Once the door had closed, she said, "There was no music box, I gather."

"No."

"A shame. Where are we going?"

"To my room. You have some explaining to do. Your brother and Robert will soon join us."

"I did go to the shops, you know. I did not lie about that."

"Let's wait until the gentlemen arrive. You don't want to have to explain things twice."

Her shoulders drooped. "Ollie seemed very angry."

"Can you blame him?" I would have said more but there was a knock on the door. Robert and Hollingsworth were on the other side.

As they walked into the room, Hollingsworth seemed more in control of himself. Walking up to his sister, he simply said, "Explain."

"I did go to the shops, Ollie, where I found Ladies Meredith and Gloria. Much like me, they were shopping for souvenirs. As the shop assistant was ringing up our purchases, Lord Harrington arrived. He was to escort them to the pier, given the fine day. They invited me to go with them."

"And you said yes."

"It seemed churlish not to do so. Lord Harrington was a perfect gentleman. Not for one second did he make me feel uncomfortable."

"He wouldn't act in an ungentlemanly manner in front of his sister," I pointed out.

"You will stay. Away. From him," Hollingsworth said through clenched teeth. So much for his calm demeanor.

Lady Mellie sighed. "I'm afraid that's not possible."

"Why the hell not?" Her brother asked.

"I'm to accompany them to the Royal Pavilion tomorrow. Lady Harrington wishes to visit it again. I couldn't get out of it, Ollie. I did try."

Hollingsworth's ire was rapidly growing out of control. But before it could erupt, I suggested, "Why don't you go with them? After all, you haven't been there. I'll ask Ned and Lady Lily to join the party as well. With all of you keeping your eye on Lord Harrington, and his mother and sister being there, he won't try anything."

Hollingsworth did not answer right away. But then he finally did. "Fine. But that's the last time you do anything with the Harringtons, Mellie. If they suggest any other activities, you'll refuse the invitation. Do I make myself clear?"

"Yes," Lady Mellie said. "Now can we please have lunch. I'm starving."

With matters settled between brother and sister, the four of us headed to The Grotto. The luncheon proved to be the calm before the storm.

CHAPTER 21

A BREWING STORM

*T*he following morning found the Harrington party, along with Lady Mellie, Hollingsworth, Ned, Lady Lily, and Lady Charlotte on their way to the Royal Pavilion. If Harrington attempted anything, he wouldn't get far.

Thinking to get a bit of private time, Robert and I had decided to take another stroll along the shore. Halfway to the pier, we encountered a familiar figure. "Father!"

"Hello, Kitty, Robert!" He was accompanied by Sir Winston, the family's basset hound.

"Taking Sir Winston for a constitutional, I see."

"He adores his walks."

Curious about a particular blue colored sea creature that lay on the sand, the basset hound attempted a sniff. But before he could do so, Father pulled him away. "Don't."

Obeying Father's command, Sir Winston put a safe distance between him and the creature.

"What is that thing?" I asked. Its transparent shade of blue resembled colored glass.

"A Portuguese Man o'War," Father said. "It has a nasty sting. They've been washing up on the shore." Gazing back at us, he asked, "Taking a break from the investigation?"

"We're waiting for the inquest at this point."

"Have you visited the pier?"

"Yes. We enjoyed something called a hot dog."

"They have sausages as well. Sir Winston loves them. Don't you, boy?"

"Woof!" Sir Winston responded. Clearly, he agreed.

"How's the investigation going?" Father asked.

"We're in the fact-finding stage right now," Robert answered. "Not enough of them to reach a conclusion at the moment."

"Well, I imagine you'll figure it out. You always do." Shading his eyes, Father gazed out to sea. "Storm clouds seem to be gathering on the horizon."

As if to affirm his statement, a wind gust suddenly came up, tossing blankets and sending beach umbrellas sailing across the sand.

"Time to return to the hotel, boy," he said to Sir Winston before gazing back at us. "See you for cocktails?"

"We'll be there."

When another strong wind blast almost bowled us over, he picked up Sir Winston and dashed toward the hotel.

"Should we also head back?" Robert asked. "The wind's getting rather nasty."

"Let's go to the pier first. I'd like a hot dog."

"Your wish is my command, milady."

Although the hot dog vendor was open for business, most other businesses were shutting down.

"Why?" I asked the vendor as I bit into the delicious sausage. "Isn't this usual weather?"

"Far from it, Miss," he said. "This one looks strong enough to take the pier with it."

Well, that was alarming. "Really?"

"Afraid so. We'd rather be safe than sorry. If the pier is damaged or destroyed, we can rebuild. But we don't dare chance getting hurt."

"That's very wise of you."

"We better go," Robert said.

I nodded.

We arrived at The Majestic to encounter sheer madness. The lobby was crammed with guests eager to check out.

Robert managed to stop a rushing porter long enough to ask. "What's going on?"

"They're forecasting a great big storm, sir. Maybe even a cyclone."

"At this time of year?"

"Yes, sir. Sorry, sir. I have to go." And off he went.

"How will everyone get out of Brighton?" I asked.

"I imagine the trains are running. At least for now. With everyone trying to leave town, it won't be easy to get seats, though. Let's check in with your family."

We found Mother writing letters in her suite.

"There's a storm bearing down on Brighton, Mother."

"Yes, sweetheart. Your father mentioned it." Always the calm in a storm.

"Where is Father?"

"With Sebastian and Margaret. He wanted to alert them about the weather situation." She glanced up. "Surely, it's not that serious."

"Have you looked out your window?" I asked.

"I have. It does appear to be a bit windy. But we're safe here, aren't we?"

"I'm not so sure, Mildred," Robert said. "Our chambers are located on the eighth floor, and they all face the sea. I believe it would be best to move to inside rooms on lower floors."

"But the hotel is full," Mother said.

"Not anymore, Mother. Guests are checking out in droves. Some rooms are bound to have opened up."

She suddenly realized the seriousness of the situation. Of course, her first thought was of her pregnant daughter. "Margaret!"

Father overheard her, as he walked in. "No need to worry, dear. She and Sebastian are aware of the situation." As a howling wind rattled the windows, he said, "But we can't stay here."

After Robert shared his suggestion, Father said, "Capital. How shall we go about this?"

"The front desk staff is too busy checking out guests. We do have a contact, though, the assistant manager. We can arrange matters with him. In the meantime, pack what you need for a couple of days."

"Surely, we won't have to be away that long," Mother said, somewhat alarmed.

"You never know how long the aftermath of the storm will last," I said. "Better be safe than sorry."

"What about the others?" Father asked. "Where are they?"

"The rest of our party is at the Royal Pavilion, except for Marlowe and Lady Emma," I said. "They were visiting the Brighton Museum and Art Gallery. Hopefully, they're all on their way back by now given the inclement weather. Mother and I can slip notes under their respective doors to let them know of our plans," I said.

"Of course, dear," Mother said.

"Hollingsworth and Lady Charlotte, expert seafarers that they are, would have realized the seriousness of the storm," Robert said. "They would have insisted on returning to the hotel."

Addressing Robert and Father, I said, "Go arrange for rooms. Let us worry about the rest of our party."

It took an hour or so, but they returned with keys to rooms on the third and fourth floors. "We'll have to do the moving ourselves. It's sheer chaos downstairs," Father said.

"We saw," I said. "The rooms won't be clean, though."

"Wouldn't be the first time I took a broom and scrub brush to a hotel chamber," Mother said.

"No need to do that, love," Father said. "I located two chambermaids and gave them hefty tips to clean those rooms. At the very least, everyone will sleep on clean linen and enjoy fresh towels."

"Well, thank heavens for that," Mother said.

"Have the others returned?" Robert asked.

"Not yet. We slipped notes under their doors."

Another wind blast rattled the windows causing them to buckle. Almost simultaneously, the electricity cut out. Although it was only midafternoon, the room had turned pitch black.

"Well, that's that," I said.

"The hotel provided candles for such emergencies, and I brought some as well," Mother said. "So we shan't be in the dark."

Mother always thought of everything. We'd already gathered about a dozen or so of them, so we lit two.

"With the electricity out, the lifts won't be working," Robert said. "We'll need to carry our own things and provide our own illumination."

Just then Margaret and Sebastian showed up at the door. "The electricity appears to have gone out," Margaret said.

"Yes, dear," Mother said. "How are you faring?"

"Fine. We're packed."

"Wonderful," Mother said. "Let us go then."

Thankfully, all we had to do was walk down. Before we

set out, we wrote another set of notes and slipped them under the doors of our friends and Ned to let them know my parents' room number. And then with Margaret lighting the way, we carefully descended the stairs. While Mother and I carried the lighter bags, Father, Robert, and Sebastian toted the trunks. Things that were not deemed important had been left behind. Once the storm passed, we could either return to our original rooms or fetch the rest of our luggage.

The third-floor chamber that had been assigned to my parents surprised me.

"This is Lady Litwell's room," I said.

"Is it really?" Mother asked lighting more candles. "Don't you need to inspect it for evidence?"

"It's already been done," Robert responded. "Catherine and I searched it. Unfortunately, we didn't find anything of note." After a momentary pause, he said, "I hope it's not disconcerting. It was the best room available. I wanted you and Edward to enjoy the most comfortable space."

"Of course not," Mother said gazing around. "Are her things still here?"

"No. Lord Litwell had them packed and moved into his quarters. Her room was cleaned by the hotel afterwards. I made sure of that."

"You think of everything, dear Robert." Glancing around, Mother said, "It is rather cozy with the candlelight."

She was taking it rather well. But then Lady Litwell was not murdered in this room. Or at least, I didn't think she'd been.

"If you will excuse me," Father said, "there's something I must check."

"Whatever could it be, Edward?" Mother asked sounding suspicious.

"Sir Winston. I want to make sure he's safe."

Rather than chide at him, she nodded. "I know you won't rest until your mind is at peace. Go."

Father wasted no time making his way out the door.

"How about some cocktails?" I asked. Father had packed our bottles of spirits in one of the trunks as he wasn't about to leave them behind.

"A little early, but I can't object," Mother said. "Robert, why don't you do the honors?"

As he started to pour libations for all, a pounding sounded on the door.

"Should be the rest of our party," Mother said.

As Robert was closest to the door, he swung it open. "Welcome to—" The rest of his words died in his throat.

I could see why. Hollingsworth stood on the other side. His face clearly edged with worry.

"What's wrong?" Robert asked.

"Mellie's gone missing."

CHAPTER 22

AN UNFORTUNATE EVENT

"What!" I said. "How did that happen?"

He stepped into the room as he started to explain. "Lord Harrington and Lady Mellie were several steps ahead of us when Lady Harrington suddenly grew faint. So, of course, we had to attend to her. By the time I glanced around, Harrington and Mellie had vanished. I wasted precious time searching for them inside the Pavilion. When I finally realized they were not there, I made my way to the cab stand in front of the building. With her red hair and his height, they were bound to attract notice. So, I asked one of the drivers if he'd seen them. He verified they'd taken a taxicab not five minutes before. How could I be so careless to take my eyes off her?" The wild-eyed look to him spoke to his agony. No wonder he was hurting. Knowing the monster Harrington was, he could very well imagine the damage the earl could inflict on his sister.

Robert must have recognized the fear in Hollingsworth

for he ordered him to sit and pushed a glass of whisky into his hand. "Drink."

Hollingsworth knocked it back in one gulp.

"Where are the others?" Mother asked.

"Right here," Ned said walking in through the open door, Ladies Lily and Charlotte by his side. "We ran into Marlowe and Lady Emma in the lobby downstairs."

"They didn't come up with you?" I asked.

"They're attending to Lady Harrington. They're trying to keep her calm. She experienced a turn when she realized her son and Lady Mellie were missing. Apparently, she suffers from a weak heart."

"Did you discover any new information about Lady Mellie?" Robert asked Ned.

"I managed to make some inquiries before heading back to the hotel. One of the drivers knows whose cab Harrington and Lady Mellie jumped into. With any luck, we'll be able to find out where he took her. I promised him a large reward if he delivered that information and the cab driver to us here at The Majestic."

"That will take too long," Hollingsworth said in a strained voice. "By the time we find her, it will be too late. He will have already . . . Damn him to hell."

Mother wisely said nothing about his language.

"I spent so many years away from my sister. And now, just as we're family once more, to have this happen to her." He brushed a trembling hand across his brow.

"He's not going to hurt her, Hollingsworth," Sebastian said. "If he does, you'll go after him, and there won't be much left. He knows that."

"So if he doesn't intend to hurt her, what does he aim to do?" Hollingsworth asked.

"Marry her, I would imagine," I said. I'd been thinking about Harrington's motives long and hard.

"Why?"

"She'd make a perfect wife for him. She's young, innocent, Catholic, his family's religion. More than that, it's what his mother wants for him. He might be a libertine, but he truly loves Lady Harrington. He probably planned this yesterday. The visit to the Royal Pavilion provided the perfect opportunity to take her."

"If he touches her, I'll kill him," Hollingsworth said through gritted teeth.

"Once they marry, there won't be anything you can do about it. The law will protect his right to his wife."

"Then we'll just have to find them before he does," Hollingsworth said a fire in his eyes. Better this than the look of despair that had been there before. "Where would he take her?"

"To London by train."

"That's a long way from the Pavilion," Margaret said. "Mellie would not go quietly. She'd scream bloody murder."

"He could have drugged her, slipped her something in the Pavilion while you were attending to his mother," I said. "It wouldn't take much to knock her unconscious."

"The dastard," Sebastian said.

"Yes, he is that and more. He probably reserved a first-class compartment so they could be private. Once they reach London, he'll take her to some secret lair of his where he'll keep her drugged until he can obtain a marriage license. And then he'd pay off a cleric with dubious morals to marry them."

"Sounds feasible," Robert said. "The railway station is as good a place to look for them. One thing he didn't count on, though, is the storm. By now, tree branches and what not have been tossed across the tracks. A train won't be departing from Brighton station anytime soon."

"Which means we have time to stop him," I said. "Father

and Sebastian can stay with Mother, Margaret, and Ladies Lily and Charlotte.

"We?" Robert shot me a searing glance. "You're not coming! In case you've forgotten, there's a storm blowing out there."

"Oh, yes, I am. Lady Mellie will need a lady in case she's incapacitated. You can't stop me, Robert."

Whatever argument he would employ next, he never used as Father rushed in through the door, clearly distraught.

"What's wrong?" Mother asked.

"Sir Winston's gone missing."

CHAPTER 23

THE CHASE

*A*s Lady Mellie's ordeal took precedence, we left the task of locating Sir Winston to the rest of our party. The drive to the Brighton Railway Station was harrowing to say the least. Although there were few cars on the road, there was plenty of debris, especially trees and branches. Thankfully there were no people. The storm had driven everyone inside.

A trip that should have taken less than fifteen minutes took half an hour as we had to constantly dodge the impediments on the road. And at one point, Hollingsworth and Robert had to step out of the taxicab we'd commandeered to clear the way. As we made our way, I had to wonder if the train had managed to leave. After all, it'd been scheduled to depart an hour ago. But Robert was probably right. The storm raged so strongly the train could not have departed. The conductor would have chosen to remain in the station until the storm passed.

Once we arrived at the railway station, we asked those milling about if they had seen a tall blonde gentleman and a red-haired lady. No one had spotted them. It didn't surprise me as crowded as the station was. As there were no more tickets to be bought, and people were clamoring to be let on the train before the storm vented its full fury on them, the station was sheer bedlam.

As we made our way up the train platform, a wind blast almost knocked me down, but Robert wrapped his arm tightly around me and helped me navigate the steps into the closest car. One of the second-class ones, as it turned out. Once he, Hollingsworth, and Ned joined me, the conductor demanded we exit the train. But when Robert flashed his credentials, he allowed us to remain aboard.

As we started the search among the second-class passengers, I spotted red hair on a woman, her head resting on a gentleman's shoulder. Strange to say the least. With the storm roaring outside, everyone was wide-awake and alert. Before I had a chance to nudge Robert, a child came tripping down the aisle holding a paper airplane in his hand, which drew the attention of the gentleman I'd spotted.

Harrington!

He jumped to his feet, clutching Mellie to him.

"The game's up, Harrington," Robert said. "Give it up."

"I don't think so." He retrieved a pistol from his pocket, pointed it straight at Robert, and fired. It didn't find its mark; it found Hollingsworth instead. He'd jumped in front of Robert.

The passengers' deafening screams filled the air as they ducked for cover. In the pandemonium, Harrington made his getaway, dragging Mellie along.

"Take care of Hollingsworth," Robert yelled at Ned and me, before going after the earl and Lady Mellie.

"Don't!" I wanted to yell, but I didn't. Hollingsworth

needed to be seen to. Fighting my panic, I knelt in the aisle where Hollingsworth lay. The bullet had caught him high on the shoulder, thankfully missing his heart. Still, it was bleeding copiously. But we were in danger of being trampled on, as everyone was rushing toward our end of the car.

Ned stood up and ordered, "Sit down. The man with the gun is gone."

"But Governor—"

"Sit!" Ned repeated.

"What if he comes back?" Someone yelled.

"He won't."

A man stood up. "You don't know that."

"The gentleman who followed him is a detective chief inspector from Scotland Yard. He'll see to it the man with the gun does not come back."

"Why keep us here?" A big brute of a man asked in a combative tone.

"You're welcome to leave. But where would you go? The storm is raging outside. We barely reached the railway station. You're safer here than out there."

As people stared out the window and each other, the clamor died down. They could see Ned was right. So did the man who challenged Ned as he retook his seat.

"Ask if there's a doctor or a nurse, Ned."

"Is there a healer on board?"

A woman raised her hand. "I'm a midwife."

"That will do."

As she quickly moved up the aisle toward us, Ned ordered the occupants of the closest seat to give it up. And then the midwife, Ned, and I gingerly took Hollingsworth and laid him across it. After one look at the wound, the midwife said, "We need bandages."

"Does anyone have bandages or clean linen?" I asked.

"I have baby nappies," a lady with a toddler on her lap answered. "Clean ones."

Beggars could not be choosers. "Bring them forward, please."

We stripped the coat off Hollingsworth and cut off his shirt. Much as Robert, he had numerous scars.

"Blimey, Miss," the lady who'd brought the nappies said. "He's been through the Great War."

"Yes, he has," I agreed. Just as likely he'd earned some during one of his seafaring adventures. And now he'd have a new one to add to his mosaic. The midwife wasted no time creating a pad of the nappies and pressing it against the wound. Once she'd done that, she wrapped another one around his shoulder to keep the pad in place. Thankfully, her ministrations worked. She'd staunched the blood.

With Hollingsworth out of immediate danger, I glanced in the direction Robert had taken. No more shots had been fired. Still, fear clawed at my gut. I had to find out what was happening with him, with Mellie. But Hollingsworth's needs came first.

Turning to the midwife, I asked, "What should we do now?"

"He needs to see a doctor. That bullet should be removed as soon as possible. Brighton General is the closest hospital."

I gazed at Ned. "Can you take him there?"

"When the storm dies down. We'd never get there now." A suspicious look grew in his eyes. "What are you going to do?"

"I'm going after them."

"Robert told you to stay put."

"I might be able to help."

"If something happens to you—"

"Nothing will happen."

He shook his head and then said, "Go. I'll take care of Hollingsworth."

I rushed in the direction Robert had taken. I didn't have far to go. They were in the luggage car, just past the second-class compartment.

Still holding a gun on Robert, Harrington had casually perched a hip on a trunk on which he'd laid Mellie. Thankfully, she was still unconscious.

"Ah, the lady fair arrives," Harrington smirked.

Without taking his eyes from him, Robert said, "Go back."

"No."

"She'll lead you a merry chase, that one. If you live long enough to marry her, that is."

"Why haven't you shot him?" I asked Harrington.

"I'm still making up my mind whether I should. He does make a tempting target."

"How's Hollingsworth?" Robert asked me.

"We stopped the bleeding."

"He lives?" Harrington asked. "That's good. At least I won't get charged with murder."

Maybe not for Hollingsworth's murder. There was still the matter of Lady Litwell. "You'll never get away with this."

"I have so far. How are you going to stop me? Need I remind you, I'm the one holding a weapon."

"What about your mother?"

"What about her?"

"She suffered a collapse at the Pavilion."

"You're lying."

"I'm not. She suffers from a heart condition, does she not?"

"How do you know that?"

"Your sister. My friends came to your mother's aid and escorted her back to the hotel. The hotel physician is seeing to her."

"She'll be fine."

"You think so? She is very upset about your disappearance. That's bound to have an effect on her heart. Why don't you give yourself up? It's not too late."

"And miss marrying Lady Melissande? She is rather lovely." He brushed a hand across the red locks that had fallen across her cheek.

"Why do you want to wed her?"

"Well, it turns out Lady Litwell filed a civil suit against me for breach of promise. Can you believe it? She wanted me to marry her stepdaughter. As if I would ever wed such a mouse."

"But she's dead. The civil suit can't move forward." Or at least I didn't think it could.

"But Lord Litwell can file another."

"Without proof, he can't force your hand."

"She had proof of other things. My peccadilloes, if you will. If they were to come out, Mother would be hurt. And that's something I wish to avoid. So, my solicitor advised me yesterday when I traveled to London that I marry and quickly. Once I did, the suit would be dropped."

"You'll never marry Lady Mellie," Robert said.

Harrington cocked his head. "You know, I think you're right. A shame. I would have enjoyed having her. Teaching her. Debauching her. Maybe I'll shoot her instead." He pressed the gun muzzle to Mellie's temple.

"If you kill her, it will destroy your mother."

"I'm afraid you're right, and I most certainly don't want that on my conscience. We're at an impasse here. Whatever shall we do?"

"Allow Catherine to take Lady Melissande. Use me as your hostage," Robert said.

"No!" I screamed. Harrington would not hesitate to shoot Robert.

"Tempting, but no. I wouldn't stand a chance against you,

Inspector. Now, Catherine—that's what you call her, isn't it? — would make a much better hostage."

"That is not happening," Robert said through clinched teeth.

"I'll do it," I said.

Robert grabbed my arm. "No, you will not."

"Ooh, a lover's quarrel," Harrington said. "How delicious! You have five seconds to decide. One, two, three."

I yanked my arm from Robert's hold and walked toward Harrington. Once I got within reach, he pulled me toward him and licked my face.

"You're disgusting!" And then I kneed him in the baubles and drove the palm of my hand up into his nose.

"You bitch!" He yelled as he crumbled to the ground, clutching his family jewels with one hand and his bleeding nose with the other.

Robert rushed forward to retrieve the weapon. Thankfully, there was some rope nearby. Robert had him trussed up in a thrice just as Mellie came around.

"What's going on?" she asked.

"Let's make our way to the other car while Robert finishes up with Lord Harrington."

"I have a raging headache," Lady Mellie said.

"Yes, love. A strong cup of tea is what you need."

CHAPTER 24

BACK AT THE HOTEL

*B*y the time Robert had finished trussing up Lord Harrington, the storm had died down to the point we could leave the station. Unfortunately for the passengers, the train was going nowhere. The tracks had to be cleared before it could proceed to London.

While Robert escorted Harrington to the Brighton Constabulary, Ned and I took Hollingsworth and Lady Mellie to Brighton General Hospital. Although the bullet was removed from Hollingsworth's shoulder, he would have to remain in the hospital for a day or so. But he would recuperate, and that's all that mattered. Lady Mellie remained woozy and suffering from a raging headache. Apparently, Harrington had chloroformed her. The hospital recommended a strong cup of tea and some sleep for her ailments.

As soon as it was feasible, we returned to The Majestic where my family and all our friends were desperate for news. After we were welcomed with glad hearts and open arms,

142

Lady Mellie was fawned over. But after the promised cup of strong tea and some food, she wanted nothing more than sleep. So, Lady Lily escorted her to their new room and tucked her in. During the long explanation, I left out some details, mainly about me playing hostage. Surely, it would have upset Mother.

Robert did not return until after ten, but I'd waited up for him. I'd eaten, bathed, and changed into my night raiment by the time he made an appearance.

"How did it go? Did he confess to Lady Litwell's murder?"

"No. That would be too much to hope for," he said, stepping into my room.

"How did he explain her state of unconsciousness?"

"He said she'd been so frightened by the storm she'd fainted."

"Total lies. He chloroformed her. How did he explain shooting Hollingsworth?""

"It was an accident. The weapon has a light trigger, apparently."

"Unbelievable. Does he really think anyone will believe that codswallop?"

"Well, you and I don't, but a jury might very well do so."

"Have you informed his mother about his whereabouts? She's been so worried."

"I stopped by her room. But she was sleeping. According to her maid, the hotel physician gave her some medication. I'll talk to her in the morning."

"Fair enough. Have you eaten?" The last thing he'd had was that hot dog at the pier. And that couldn't have kept him satisfied until now.

"Beans, hot buttered toast, a cup of tea."

"Not much of a meal."

"I've had worse, and sometimes gone without."

"I had the kitchen bring up a fruit and cheese tray. All

they could manage given the circumstances." I pointed to the covered dish on the round table near us. "There's no tea, just water."

"Water will do. Thank you, Catherine."

I plated the cut fruit and cheese and placed it in front of him. While he had his fill, I enjoyed the sight of him. "We've barely had a moment to ourselves this entire holiday. But now, just the two of us, it's rather cozy, isn't it?" We were alone in a room lit only by candlelight.

"Indeed, it is, sweetheart." He captured my hand and kissed it.

"I wish. I wish . . ." I allowed the thought to dangle in the air.

"What do you wish?" He asked softly.

"That we could spend the night together." There. I'd said it. And I wasn't sorry. I meant every word.

He brushed back the lock of hair that had fallen across my face. "I wouldn't be much of a gentleman if I laid with you tonight." He leaned toward me and kissed me. "Our wedding night will come soon enough."

I shot him a disgruntled look "Not soon enough!"

His lips shaped into an amused smile. "Oh, my darling Catherine. How I do love you."

I pulled back from him. "You're awful."

Now openly laughing, he came to his feet. "And with that tender expression of your love, I'll take my leave."

I allowed him to take several steps before I said, "Wait!"

He turned back to me.

"Let's have our morning meal here tomorrow. Just the two of us. I'll order room service." Hopefully, the electricity would be restored by then so the kitchen could serve us a hot breakfast.

He pinched my chin, a loving gesture of his. "What time?"

"Nine?"

"Nine, it is."

He turned back toward the door.

"You don't have to leave that way."

He turned around once more. "Catherine."

"No. It's not that." I took his hand and led him to another door, the one between our rooms.

"Our rooms connect?"

"Yes, and Mother doesn't know," I whispered as I opened the door. "I'll leave it unlocked." I wrapped my arms around his waist and kissed him the way he always kissed me. After slowly ending it, I pushed him into his room. "Dream of me, Inspector," and then I shut the door in his face. The look in his eyes was one I would treasure for a long, long time.

The following morning dawned bright and clear, a perfect jewel of a day. But then that's often the way after a storm. Even better the electricity had been restored which hopefully meant things would return to at least a semblance of normal. Sure enough, when I telephoned room service and asked for breakfast for two to be delivered at nine, the hotel employee simply took the order.

I'd just finished dressing when there was a knock on the door. If that was breakfast, it was a tad early. It was only a quarter to nine. Indeed, that proved to be the case. I didn't complain. They probably had their hands full at the moment. I just hoped Robert arrived soon so his food wouldn't get cold.

Not a minute after the server left, another knock sounded on the door. Grace opened it to find Lady Esther on the other side.

"There's something I wish to discuss." She glanced at the

table on which the breakfast service rested. "I'm interrupting your breakfast. Maybe I should go."

"Nonsense. I have a few minutes. Come in."

We waited until Grace had left before she opened up. "I'm afraid I wasn't totally truthful with you."

"Oh? What about?"

"My trip to London."

"To visit a physician."

"Yes. It was not a minor complaint."

"What was the reason then?"

"My stepmama thought I was increasing."

So my reasoning had been correct. "And were you?"

"No. I was merely late, that's all."

"Why would she think you were pregnant?"

"Lord Harrington. When he visited our estate last year, he seduced me."

Dear heaven! "He didn't . . . force you, did he?"

"No. I was willing. It happened only once. I was just a diversion. He left without saying goodbye."

I pressed her hands. "I'm so sorry. How did Lady Litwell discover your courses were late?"

"My maid told her. A creature not to be trusted."

"Absolutely. You need to dismiss her."

"I already have," she said with a curl to her lip.

"What did Lady Litwell do once she found out?"

"She pressed me for the whole story. I'm ashamed to admit I broke down."

It was no wonder she had. Lady Litwell had such a strong personality. Lady Esther could have never stood up to her.

"The next day we were on our way to London. Overnight she'd devised an entire blackmail scheme against Lord Harrington. If I were pregnant, she would use it to force him to marry me. When that proved not to be the case, she decided to proceed with her plan anyway. She had proof that he'd debauched an innocent."

"What proof?"

"I kept his Rose and Thistle pin. The night he came to me, he was drunk. Fell asleep the moment he . . ."

"You don't have to continue. I understand."

"So I stole it. I knew what it represented. Oscar told me."

"Your brother didn't . . . belong to that same club, did he?"

"Oh, no. Oscar prefers men. The Rose and Thistle members only debauch women, some much younger than me."

"But if you knew this, why did you invite him to your room?"

"I wanted to know what it felt like. I thought it would be glorious." Her expression turned angry. "But it wasn't. It was degrading and messy and it hurt. He didn't even remember my name. I was nothing but a vessel for him to slake his lust."

"Did he agree to marry you?"

"No. He laughed at my stepmother. I was too homely, too simple. And I possessed no dowry. Plus, I was Church of England, and his family is Catholic. My stepmother told him she would dower me. He told her he would need proof. That was last November. She not only had her solicitor draw up a document, but she included the bequest in her will. In March at the start of the season, she showed it to him and demanded that our engagement be announced. He flat-out refused."

"Why was Lady Litwell so keen to have you marry him?"

"More than anything, she wants to be accepted by the aristocracy. Her marriage to my father helped her gain entry, but not acceptance. The Harrington title is one of the oldest in England. If I became Lady Harrington, they would have to accept her as one of them. Or so she determined."

"What did she do when Harrington refused?"

"She had him investigated. Once she found his weakness, she knew what she needed to do."

"What is his weakness?" I knew what it was, but I needed her to say it.

"His mother. She doesn't know he debauches women, some as young as twelve, or the nasty games he likes to play. And my stepmother obtained proof. His mother has a weak heart. If she learned what her son has done, she might very well die."

"That's what she held over his head?"

"Yes. When presented with that evidence, he agreed to marry me."

So, Harrington had lied on the train. "But the plan went wrong somehow."

"Yes." There was a rather nasty smile on her face. "Stepmama arranged for him to come to her room to sign the betrothal agreement. Once his signature was on that document, he couldn't back out, you see."

"Did he in fact come to her room?"

"Oh, yes. That's when he killed her."

I gasped. "How do you know he killed her?"

"Silly question. I was in the room, of course."

"You saw him kill her?"

"Yes." The nasty smile grew wider.

"But you didn't say anything?"

"Why would I?"

"Because he murdered your stepmother."

"Good riddance. All she did was harp at me. Don't you see? She had to go." There was a mad light in her eyes.

She was insane. How had I not seen this before? "Did you know he meant to murder her?"

"Know? Miss Worthington, I planned the whole thing," she cackled.

"You arranged for him to kill her?"

"Yes."

"Why?"

"She arranged a marriage to a man who would most surely abuse me. She only cared about herself and her social standing. And then there was all that lovely money. She showed me the will, you know, told me I needed all the help I could get to get married. That no man would look twice at me. I was homely, had no grace, no airs. I couldn't string two sentences together without tripping over my words." Lady Esther hitched up her chin. "Well, I showed her. With fifty thousand pounds, I won't have to depend on anyone. I can go live in the south of France and spend my days painting. And after France, Italy, Greece. The world will be my oyster."

"What would Harrington get out of murdering Lady Litwell?" I had to hear spell it out.

"He wouldn't have to marry me, of course. He could keep doing all those things he likes to do. Disgusting as they are."

"Why are you confessing all this to me?"

That seemed to take her by surprise. "Oh, I'm not confessing. He killed her, not me."

"But you planned it along with him. You're just as guilty as he is."

That took her aback. "No, I'm not."

"I'm afraid the law will see it that way, Lady Esther." How could she be so naive?

She narrowed her gaze. "Well, no one will know because you're not going to tell."

"I'm afraid I am. I must."

"No, you won't." And with that she snatched the knife from the breakfast service and flew at me knocking me over. With her getting the upper hand, it took everything in me to stop her from plunging the blade into my breast.

The connecting door opened and Robert strolled in.

"Catherine, I—" One look and he rushed forward to haul Lady Esther to her feet.

With a furious look in her eyes, she turned and stabbed at him. She didn't get far as he didn't hesitate to clip her jaw. She landed on the carpet with a thud.

After he took the knife from her hand, he helped me to my feet. "What on earth's going on?"

"She dreamed up the scheme for Lord Harrington to kill Lady Litwell. She planned the whole thing."

CHAPTER 25

DENOUEMENT

*L*ady Esther was in a combative mood, so Robert had no choice but to put handcuffs on her. Thankfully, he traveled with them as he never knew when a situation might arise. After he'd secured her, he put a call through to the Brighton Constabulary. A half hour later, the Superintendent and Constable Brown arrived. A brief discussion later, they led Lady Esther down the corridor to the lift, with Robert and I trailing them. Lady Esther did not go quietly. She screamed like a banshee the entire way. Doors up and down the hallway crashed open. Guests, most of whom were my family and friends, stuck out their heads. Thankfully, Lord Litwell was not one of them.

"What's going on?" Mother asked.

"I'll explain later." Once we exited the hotel, the Superintendent and Constable Brown helped Lady Esther into a police car. Robert and I followed them in a taxicab. Since

Lady Esther had confessed to me, I would need to provide a statement.

At the Brighton constabulary, she was advised to remain silent until a solicitor could be obtained for her. Instead of doing so, she continued to assert her innocence, while providing facts only she and the murderer would know. In the end, she was tossed into the jail cell next to Harrington's who proceeded to berate her and call her unspeakable names. After I gave my statement, Robert and I returned to the hotel hoping against hope to salvage what was left of our holiday.

Unfortunately, that was not to be. The hotel had suffered so much storm damage, the Majestic could not house guests. We spent the rest of the morning packing so we could catch the late afternoon train to London. Father had been happily reunited with Sir Winston. Turned out the hotel staff member in charge of the kennels had moved him and two other pooches to his room for safekeeping.

As we couldn't very well leave Hollingsworth behind, Robert attended to that task. Amidst all the chaos, the hotel managed to serve us a splendid luncheon in the hotel restaurant. As we were practically the last guests still there, we were fawned over and feted by them. A few members of the hotel band even made an appearance. They played their hearts out, somehow capturing the magic of that first night.

Lady Harrington, after being informed of her son's arrest, had suffered another turn. This one was so bad she had to be admitted to Brighton General Hospital where she would hopefully recuperate. Lady Meredith couldn't very well be left alone. But thankfully, the Harringtons had family nearby, so they arrived in the early afternoon to take custody of her until other arrangements could be made.

And then finally, it was time to depart. Even with all the insanity that had transpired, I was sad to leave Brighton.

There was something magical about a holiday at the shore. We'd managed to capture it. For a time, anyway.

Seemingly reading my thoughts, Robert said, "We'll return darling. Once we're married."

"Promise?"

"I do."

A week later life had by and large returned to normal. At least for us. Margaret and Sebastian had settled into their London mansion before heading to Oxford in September. Although she'd assured Sebastian she was hale and hearty, he wished for her to spend the next month or so in a calm environment before she became involved in her Oxford recruiting endeavors. Believing she owed him for the way she'd treated him, Margaret acquiesced. But nothing would keep her from traveling to Oxford in September.

Hollingsworth had bounced back from his injury with amazing alacrity. But he'd decided to remain in London rather than return to Bristol to oversee the fitting of his ship. Lady Mellie seemed hardly fazed by her ordeal which I suppose made sense since she'd spent most of it unconscious. At home, she happily resumed her piano playing, buying sheet music and practicing popular tunes. Something all who resided at Worthington House enjoyed. Lady Lily and Ned had settled on a date for their wedding. They would marry next June. Marlowe and Lady Emma continued their bickering which was a comfort of sorts. They wouldn't argue so much if they didn't care about one another. Sir Winston took up his usual spot in the kitchen where he was fawned over by the kitchen staff, especially Cook who fed him a continuous diet of his beloved sausages. Mother and Father returned to their daily lives with little change except for one thing. Once a week, they dined alone in Mother's bedroom suite. I was happy to see them rekindle their love. I could only hope

Robert and I would enjoy that kind of closeness in our golden years.

Two weeks after our return to London, word reached us that Lady Harrington had sadly passed away. Once her son's full perfidy became known, her heart had given out at last. At least she was spared the final indignity. As a peer, Harrington would not be tried in a common court of law, but in the House of Lords. His charm would cut no ice with that august body. More than likely, he would hang for Lady Litwell's murder.

Lady Esther was another story altogether. Although she'd planned the murder, she was the daughter of an earl and, more importantly, a minor. Lord Litwell hired a solicitor who framed her seduction as rape as she lacked the capacity to give consent. He also argued she was unfit to plea as she did not understand the crime she'd committed. As evidence, he used Lady Esther's ramblings to me.

When the scandal hit the papers, the public quickly took her side, especially when Lord Harrington's deviant behavior came to light. He was branded the villain, while she was seen as a victim. Eager to put the whole matter behind them, the Crown Prosecution Service opted not to charge Lady Esther. However, she would not get the money her stepmother had left her and would remain under the supervision of her father until such time she was deemed capable.

Once that decision was reached, Lord Litwell promptly placed her under medical supervision in a Cotswolds sanatorium where she would enjoy fresh air, good food, and not much else. I doubted she would be released any time soon, as she was something he'd rather forget. Even if she'd not been given a jail sentence, her life would be hell on earth.

And as for Robert and me, we were glad to be back in London. With our wedding day only two months away, I was soon dealing with fittings for my trousseau, wedding invitations, and a thousand other things.

On the delivery date of our wedding china, silverware, and glassware to his Eaton Square address, I made sure Robert would be present, as I wanted to see his expression when he saw them firsthand.

I'd, of course, alerted his staff. But my arrival was a surprise to him.

"Catherine," he kissed my cheek. "I didn't know you were coming."

I grinned. "I wanted to surprise you."

"And a pleasant surprise it is. Any special reason you came to visit?"

He knew me so well. "Our wedding china has been delivered."

"Has it?"

"Yes, along with the silverware and glassware. I wanted to see your expression when you first saw them."

"Where is it?" he asked glancing around.

"In the dining room. Cook has prepared a special dinner for us which I hope you'll enjoy."

"I'm sure I will."

"Now close your eyes." When he did, I led him into the dining room where everything had been arranged. "You can open them now."

The china, glassware, and flatware all glistened from the light of the chandelier.

"It's beautiful," he said.

"You haven't examined them yet." I picked up the dinner plate and showed it to him. "It's bone china with a platinum rim and silver flourishes around the perimeter." A pair of small silver swans, their long necks forming a heart, adorned the top of the plate.

I pointed them out. "It's a symbol of our love. Do you like it?"

He smiled softly at me. "It's perfect. Just like you."

And then he kissed me, and the whole world went away.

~

DID you enjoy A Murder at Brighton? Read on to discover Kitty's next adventure.

Murder at a Funeral

England. 1924. With her wedding day to **Chief Detective Inspector Robert Crawford Sinclair** mere weeks away, **Kitty Worthington** is thrilled beyond words. But first there's a sad duty that must be performed—the reinterment of Robert's birth mother at Castle Rutledge. She is to be buried alongside her husband, the former marquis.

But on the day of the funeral, things don't go according to plan. The vicar's gone missing; the organist is drunk as a judge. And then there's the body in the sanctuary. Not the one you'd expect.

The village constable soon asks Robert to help, something that Kitty advises against, afraid of the emotional toll the enquiry would exact on her fiancé. But then Lord Rutledge, Robert's brother, is suspected of the crime, leaving them with no choice but to investigate.

Goodness knows they're not lacking for suspects. The village crone caused endless strife in Chipping Bliss. As they proceed apace, shocking revelations and troubled pasts come to light. And just as they discover a vital clue, a threatening note arrives. If they don't cease their investigation, a loved one will die.

Murder at a Funeral, Book 9 in The Kitty Worthington

Mysteries, is an enthralling mystery sure to delight lovers of Agatha Christie and the golden age of mysteries. Available on Amazon.

∾

HAVE you read the first Kitty Worthington Mystery? **Murder on the Golden Arrow**, Book 1 in the Kitty Worthington Mysteries, is available on Amazon and Kindle Unlimited

What's a bright young woman to do when her brother becomes the main suspect in a murder? Why, solve the case of course.

England. 1923. After a year away at finishing school where she learned etiquette, deportment, and the difference between a salad fork and a fish one, Kitty Worthington is eager to return home. But minutes after she and her brother Ned board the Golden Arrow, the unthinkable happens. A woman with a mysterious connection to her brother is poisoned, and the murderer can only be someone aboard the train.

When Scotland Yard hones in on Ned as the main suspect, Kitty sets out to investigate. Not an easy thing to do while juggling the demands of her debut season and a mother intent on finding a suitable, aristocratic husband for her.

With the aid of her maid, two noble beaus, and a flatulent basset hound named Sir Winston, Kitty treads a fearless path through the glamorous world of high society and London's dark underbelly to find the murderer. For if she fails, the insufferable Inspector Crawford will most surely hang a noose around her brother's neck.

Murder on the Golden Arrow, Book 1 in The Kitty Worthington Mysteries. A historical cozy mystery filled with dodgy suspects, a dastardly villain, and an intrepid heroine sure to win your heart. Available on Amazon and Kindle Unlimited.

ISBN-13: 978-1-943321-24-7 (EBook)

ISBN-13: 978-1-943321-33-9 (Paperback)

Hearts Afire Publishing

First Edition

Made in the USA
Middletown, DE
31 December 2023

47024753R00099